Twenty Years on Graysheep Bay

Twenty Years on Graysheep Bay

A Microcosmic Look at a Macrocosm of Human and Natural Life: Chesapeake Bay

Ray Greenblatt

SUNSTONE
PRESS

SANTA FE

Sunstone books may be purchased for educational, business, or sales promotional use.
For information please write: Special Markets Department, Sunstone Press,
P.O. Box 2321, Santa Fe, New Mexico 87504-2321.
Body typeface › Adobe Caslon Pro
Printed on acid-free paper
∞
eBook 978-1-61139-494-8

Library of Congress Cataloging-in-Publication Data

Names: Greenblatt, Ray, author.
Title: Twenty years on Graysheep Bay : a microcosmic look at a macrocosm of
  human and natural life : Chesapeake Bay / by Ray Greenblatt.
Description: Santa Fe, N.M. : Sunstone Press, 2017.
Identifiers: LCCN 2016046449 (print) | LCCN 2016059080 (ebook) | ISBN
  9781632931597 (softcover : acid-free paper) | ISBN 9781611394948
Subjects: LCSH: Chesapeake Bay (Md. and Va.)--Fiction. | Interpersonal
  relations--Fiction. | City and town life--Fiction.
Classification: LCC PS3557.R37895 T94 2017 (print) | LCC PS3557.R37895
  (ebook) | DDC 813/.54--dc23
LC record available at https://lccn.loc.gov/2016046449

SUNSTONE PRESS IS COMMITTED TO MINIMIZING OUR ENVIRONMENTAL IMPACT ON THE PLANET. THE PAPER USED IN THIS BOOK IS FROM
RESPONSIBLY MANAGED FORESTS. OUR PRINTER HAS RECEIVED CHAIN OF CUSTODY (COC) CERTIFICATION FROM: THE FOREST STEWARDSHIP
COUNCIL™ (FSC®), PROGRAMME FOR THE ENDORSEMENT OF FOREST CERTIFICATION™ (PEFC™), AND THE SUSTAINABLE FORESTRY INITIATIVE® (SFI®).
THE FSC® COUNCIL IS A NON-PROFIT ORGANIZATION, PROMOTING THE ENVIRONMENTALLY APPROPRIATE, SOCIALLY BENEFICIAL AND
ECONOMICALLY VIABLE MANAGEMENT OF THE WORLD'S FORESTS. FSC® CERTIFICATION IS RECOGNIZED INTERNATIONALLY AS A
RIGOROUS ENVIRONMENTAL AND SOCIAL STANDARD FOR RESPONSIBLE FOREST MANAGEMENT.

WWW.SUNSTONEPRESS.COM
SUNSTONE PRESS / POST OFFICE BOX 2321 / SANTA FE, NM 87504-2321 /USA
(505) 988-4418 / ORDERS ONLY (800) 243-5644 / FAX (505) 988-1025

To my wife, Sue

Contents

Preface

This book did take twenty years to bake, as in the actual title. All that time I was unconsciously gathering ingredients. It takes time to get to know people; then to enter into their customs. I found that even the local architecture held its uniquenesses: private homes, restaurants, and the singularity of each small shore town.

All the while the Bay lay quietly—and sometimes roughly—observing all events. I found that humans effected the Bay, but more often it colored their moods and decisions. I knew a man like Hap (all characters in a book are a composite); his life hinged on how the water was acting on a certain day. Frank Russo was enthralled by the mystique of the sea, the Hemingway macho fisherman he pursued. And poor thwarted Chip ended up facedown floating in a marina slip.

So many people are influenced in different ways by their environment. When I decided to write the book, I took the unusual step to look at several people instead of just a few, or a family. These brief but hopefully telling glances capture a significant moment in that person's life. I did not feel out of step because a new style of prose writing, Flash Fiction, has been evolving for several years.

Along the same line of thinking, I selected short poems to capture a momentary interaction, often with the Bay. The shortness—even fragmentation—serves best to capture a key moment of emotion. In addition, I wanted to have a poem echo a prose passage. Also, in this experimental mode I included letters, lists, diary jottings to emphasize the quick instances of human action or thought.

Humans are the most important element in this book. Some battle difficulties and survive; others are not so fortunate. As the Bay is a constant protagonist and shaper of men, so are the seasons. But it can't all be sturm und drang. We must laugh at Virginia who hears eighteenth century fife and drum through the water pipes; or Daisy who talks to a seafaring ghost. Man has chosen to live by the water over his long history. These reasons are fundamental: an interdependence with the sea is inherent in our DNA.

—Ray Greenblatt

The Ideal Couple

Helen had legs that—some would-be connoisseurs said—went on forever. Her skin was cream and butter. But her eyes would creep into you. Then, at some odd moment, they would shift and float away over the horizon, you only fearing they would never return.

Helen grew up in the country in the middle of a bunch of siblings. Early on everyone in the small town knew she would be an artist. Her mother would call her for breakfast and find her daydreaming on the half-made bed. She drew scenes on her walls and made clothes from miscellaneous, brightly colored remnants.

There are two kinds of Scout leaders: the young, handsome one with a lot of forthright courage; the other, a patient listener. Stewart was the latter. Bald headed, with rimless glasses, snaggle-toothed—and yet the scouts were drawn to him.

Helen and Stewart ended up in the same large advertising firm in Manhattan. Two small town persons, they both discovered the dynamism of the metropolis. As time went on, with hit and miss hints from mutual friends, they found each other. People around them considered them hippies, at least compared to anyone else in that middleclass environment.

Yes, the money was good. Helen and Stewart got married and found an apartment big enough for both of them. But it took a lot of their combined incomes not only to exist but to enjoy the cultural benefits they both loved.

It wasn't many years before the work routine began to wear them down. Stewart could still find some time to do the creative writing he had always loved. And Helen? An art gallery; but where was a field of spring flowers. A new restaurant; but where were woods where fresh mushrooms could be picked. Helen grew so depressed she had trouble getting out of bed in the morning; her sick days were quickly exhausted.

The death of Uncle Stephen came like a godsend. He had left a cabin on the Bay to Stewart's father. However, the father did not want it and decided to pass it on to his son as part of his youngest's inheritance.

By the end of the year Helen and Stewart had quit their jobs and were wished good luck and a fulfilled destiny by their friends. Stewart remembered the quaint building beside the water. He had fished and canoed there with his family when a teenager. Helen just wanted the peace and quietness of the setting; urban cultural benefits she had left behind.

But Uncle Stephen had become a recluse in later years. The cabin now needed a new roof, insulation, a better heating system. Stewart was no longer content with the outhouse he had found an adventure when a kid.

They bought self-help books and brought all their skills to bear. To supplement their dwindling nest egg, Stewart did come freelance writing and consulting; his serious writing would have to come later. Helen designed note paper and postcards that local shops, though few, were happy to take on consignment.

That was a few years ago. They seem to be content, they're still working on the cabin—which they insist on calling a house, but it's coming along.

Spring Piping

Swathes of gray on ridges
against a faded blue,
trees stripped and gnarled, shadow of
the house—its knobs and nooks—
nearly fills in the lawn.
Although movement of reeds
sounds harsh and sapless,
late sun tamed, the piping
in the marshes begins.
Sporadic hammering
beyond the hill suggests
people thinking about
the outdoors, the sprawled garden.

When?

When is the best time an author should start his book? In winter we are all closed in. The world becomes mightily small; a good time to concentrate. Or in spring you feel a new growth; what better time to birth a bit of writing. Perhaps autumn when you sense things slipping away, dying; get it down before it's too late.

I began to write in summer, the impossible time to concentrate. Sweat drips onto your paper. You keep blinking as thoughts mush in your brain. I began to write smack in the middle of summer—July 15, I remember—because it was my birthday. No other reason, perhaps celebration of some sort, I'm not really sure. After so many birthdays you soon want to forget them. I started to write.

But when I tried to write, I couldn't. I knew I had loads of material; I had been churning it over for years, developing ideas even in my sleep. But strange things began to happen. I could feel my teeth grinding, my hands shook, I was even sweating. I couldn't believe my own responses.

My glasses had to be cleaned. I told myself that I couldn't think straight if my hair was not combed. Was the temperature of the room comfortable? the chair? Did I have enough cool drinking water by me?

Had I finished reading a book with no other to immediately pick up. Had I exhausted listening to the music CDs I had bought. I told myself that I had the entire day before my interesting night TV would start. Proper paper, proper pen, adequate clipboard. I couldn't work in front of an awkward computer screen, at least not the first draft. I needed to feel, to write organically if I was going to tell about real life. The mechanization of second or third rewrite would follow soon enough.

You see, with all of these phobias, I could postpone indefinitely.

But eventually something got to me. Maybe the guilt built up high enough to push me into it.

Stimulus

All I have and everything
I have to write about
is liquid. Watermen
make a living here and
most others feed upon them,
even vacationers
spend their energy
beneath sky above sea.
Dip of gull into the Bay
like a glance of a sail or
paper caught in a current
is what nourishes
and feels fresh each day.

Location, Location

Our motive was to invest in a house for our retirement. Actually we both were missing the water, having grown up near it. We felt even a weekend there would refresh us. We had experienced the restful feeling in a B&B by the shore; now we wanted our own house.

On a series of weekends when we could get away long enough from our jobs, we began to hunt for a house to the south. But that was where the fashionable people went, we soon discovered. We couldn't afford the land, let alone a house on it.

Working our way slowly north along the Bay, we learned that we wanted a place with a view of the water. But not a flat view—that is, hills and woods were necessary. This was becoming too much of a challenge on our own, so we engaged a real estate agent, a woman who had been in the business a long time.

House after house was available, but we always found some flaw. Was it just our problem? The weekends turned into work. One weekend my wife exclaimed: "This house is perfect, it's a decent price, and I can see the water!" She was standing on one leg peering around the corner of the porch at distant glints through some trees.

Another time our agent had been trying to find a certain house in a small neighborhood. My tired wife decided to stay in the van. The agent tried the door, found it unlocked, and we looked through the rooms. She got on her cell phone to her office to discover it was not the house we wanted. I could imagine a shotgun as we hurriedly escaped!

That night we thought things over once again. "Look," I reasoned, "let's just buy some land with the hope of building in the future. That's all we can afford."

We decided that our house would have to be a small one, so we talked to a local builder. We accepted an offer for a piece of land attached to a larger piece of property. Before we went to the signing our lawyer noticed there was no entrance or exit. We would have to come in by helicopter! That was the end of that deal.

One day we saw our builder's sale sign on some property near the

Bay. I phoned him. "Hey, I thought you only built houses and didn't sell property. "

"I do both. You didn't ask me."

So that's how we came to live north of where we began our grand search and why we live in a small house—but it has a water view!

Spring Tide

Ring of fog makes our sea
village exclusive.
Silent beachcomber
with elastic spine,
silent gardener
deep in her overgrown plot.
Tree stump detaches
itself to become
lone heron flapping away,
sparrow crowns each reed
with a melody.
Pairs of ducks throughout the town,
high tide swells the earth.

Hap

If the name Hap ever comes up, I immediately think of curly hair under a cap, fishing vest, permanently red forearms and back of the neck. Hap knows all the spots along the Bay, up the rivers and streams and tributaries. He can tell you when a dam will discharge, how severe the spring thaw might be, and how the rockfish are running. He somehow finds time from fishing to make a living. At what I don't know. For a waterman who must be quiet while fishing, Hap is a talker.

"I went up to Maine once. Went mackerel trolling with a pal who moved up there. We went out in his dinghy. Five hooks on a line. We went motoring around looking for a school when, Bam—one, two, three! We pulled in our lines to find every hook held a dark shiny fish. Well, that was an easy catch, but somehow you pay for what you do. As we're putting toward the dock, I happen to look behind me. Jeezus, a huge surge of wave was following us. Give it all it's got, Mort! I yelled. He nearly tore that outboard off the stern. But we made it somehow. Fish ate good too.

"Tried warm water once. Florida. Never do it again. Can you picture me with a spear gun, mask, flippers. Jeez, I felt like a Martian. Couldn't believe we were swimming with barracuda. But that water was so clear. Something I'd like up here. We were near the bottom, maybe twenty feet down, when a giant shadow passed over. I thought for sure a shark. I pulled up short and my feet caught some sea urchins lying on the sand. Man, I needed tweezers to get those suckers out. Stung like hell.

"But if you're going to do real deep-sea fishing, you should go out in a hired boat. Those guys have all the instruments for finding wrecks and such where fish gather. Swap stories with old timers. Feel like you're in the middle of nowhere. As the boat pitches, watching greenhorns puke over the side is diverting too. Then bite into a thick pickle sandwich and watch them heave all over again."

Day's Vigor

We seem breathless all day
energized, doing really
nothing—meals, cleaning up
garden, tossing newspapers
until we find ourselves
on the beach and allow
the natural do to us;
her eyes gleaming, sometimes
bit of kick in her step,
not us scarred by love;
grand climax of the day is
orange glare off window,
tabletop, floor plank.

Architecture

Let's take a stroll around town and I'll show you some sights. That long thin clapboard house reminds me of a Boy Scout headquarters; I guess it's the bunkhouse effect. An old Greek couple live there. He had a small retail business and retired a few years ago. They take good care of the house, but you seldom see them outside, even on the porch. Lights often burn late in the rear of the building away from the Bay. They are proud of their heritage and have talked for years about going back to the old country to live. But they are running out of time.

Look closely at that house. See how the central part of it is brick. But wings were added to both sides and the entire structure painted white. It used to be a gun club. Matter of fact, a legend lingers that a Continental lady in gray walks up and down the stairs with a candle at midnight. People from DC own it now. He is an engineer. She just seems to collect dolls; nice enough person, but she claims to take care of their vast garden herself yet is never outside. They showed much generosity sharing food from their reserve freezers with townsfolk when the electric went out in the worst hurricane this region has ever known.

That's a handsome Victorian house on the hill. It's huge but has only one bathroom—on the first floor at that. I've never been inside but somebody told me it's jammed with antiques. A gay couple in California who inherited it come once a year to stay a few weeks and inspect it. Why don't they sell it or make it into a B & B; it would be a natural.

I like that house built just a few years ago. It has a relaxed southern look to it. Low with long windows, even ceiling fans on the outside veranda. A wine merchant, who grew up in this town, came back to settle down with his young family; getting away from the rat race. Built living quarters for the grandparents over the garage. After a while the wife decided the schools in the area weren't good enough for her kids. They moved back to suburbia.

Yes, you can call that yellow pile a McMansion. It must have cost millions to build. It sits in the lowest part of town where the water collects in storms. They've raised the house on pilings. It hasn't been here long enough to be really tested. Everybody is waiting.

Swamp Tortoise

She was dusty but
her eyes were liquid and bright.
Lately the swamp water
had spread like an announcement.
Now she was digging
a row of shallow holes
deciding which would house
decoys, which offspring.
She rested in pale spring sun
surveying her dirt strip
so dutifully worked.
She soon would disappear but
her handiwork would multiply.

Ambience

Agood place to eat breakfast is The Blue Whale. Some people call it The Aquarium because the front is curved chrome and inset blue plastic panels; like the diners from World War Two.

Food is plentiful; they serve breakfast, lunch, dinner. But breakfast is best. They put a spin on regular dishes: hints of lemon in the pancakes, waffles in the shapes of animals dazzle kids, and morsels you can't identify in the omelets but they're succulent. The regulars are at the counter—Ernie, Dekes, Al, Munchy—mostly watermen. The coffee, a secret blend, knocks you out.

The star is undoubtedly Louise. As big as her owner mother is petite, Louise has waited tables since she was eleven. She can memorize orders for a table of twelve. Louise has everything: bows in her hair and tattoos; blue eyes like stars, freckles, dimples. She gets around the tables as fast as a pinball. She can swap jokes—not always clean—with the fastest of them. Nobody knows what they will do when she goes off to community college next fall.

A place to go especially in winter is McKay's Café. It's like walking into the Admiral Benbow Inn in Treasure Island. Wooden floor creaks at every step. Wooden walls shiver if a wind hits them. Best to sit near the Franklin stove and watch raindrops distort the flapping plastic over the windows.

Charlotte is the queen of this establishment. Her body is a hickory plank turned on a lathe; her eyes set so far back behind her spectacles it looks as if they're hiding in caves. The going challenge is to make Charlotte laugh; as far as I know, no one has yet won. The hamburgers are real meat, large, greasy, and delicious. A powerful rum & coke tops the meal off.

The best quality food in the area is found at the St. Hortense Inn. The view of the Bay is almost 270 degrees. The food is served with real style—what is now called "presentation." They tried to hype it up with a real calypso band from Trinidad. It didn't go over. I don't know why they ever tried. They've got a great Swiss chef; the prices are reasonable. Their view is the best around; they face a state park so it will always be green across the Bay, with not one light blinking at night.

There are many other places to eat of varied quality and reputation. It depends on your mood at the time. The Rochester has a second floor balcony where college kids with a beer too many—the owners make their own brew in the warehouse next door—drop dinner rolls on their friends walking by below.

A biker bar sits in the loblollies. A 6'8" ex-wrestler is the bartender and owner. Photos on the wall go back to Gorgeous George and Andre the Giant. A twisted Turkish towel soaked in water is used on the rowdy guests. A short pair of Filipino twins drag the customer out just in time to meet the arriving state troopers.

Two ladies started a tea room. They rented a wing of an old wandering house in Willowdale and put in little round tables. They learned some British recipes for scones, meat pies, pastries. That, nice silverware, and tea in English porcelain pots have made their fame. They sometimes have a trio play chamber music or a tenor sing ballads.

Eden Turns

We slept naked on the back porch
in the hammock of summer,
morning dew oiled our skin
breeze's warm lips served us,
water sang in gentle ripples
scent of sea mint circled the house.
Then weather's wicked whip
descended curdling all sweetness,
the skin of our house trembled
roaring surf stuffed ears
brimstone lurked in gray seas,
as key causeways swamped and
we were choked up to the neck.

The House Next-Door

The history of the house next-door spirals into the gloom of failure. A young couple with a load of kids lived there. They were best known around the neighborhood for owning seven Husky pups. People young and old came over to watch them romp in the fenced in yard.

One cold autumn day a neighbor noticed their back door swinging open. Children's toys were still in the yard, dogs gone too, the house empty. Turned out the family was trying to outrun the mortgage company.

A middle-aged couple moved in next. He had been making a comfortable living as an electrician in the city. But the beauty of the Bay called to them. Being handy he even added a wing to the house. He became an investor in a local restaurant and she joined the zoning board. Some grew to dislike her letter of the law, but she said she only wanted to keep the town as nice as it was.

As time went on, he realized that an electrician in a small town could not get the work he was used to. He had been a union man which got him lots of contracts. Having trouble making ends meet, they returned to the city, vowing they would return. Nobody has seen them since.

Recently an extended family moved in. Extended can mean a lot of different things these days. You can extend all that you want, but with children involved, a risk to life would be the line one would not cross. I noticed one of the children cutting the backyard with a gasoline mower. This is good because it teaches youngsters skills and self-reliance. However, for fun he was pouring the gas from can to grass while lighting it.

This kind of crazy game could burn not only him but the woods behind our houses. I yelled at him, ran and pounded on their front door to warn some adult. A bleary-eyed grandmother cracked open the door a bit and snarled at me. I told her the facts. "Yeah, I know," she said, " we've told him to stop it," and closed the door on me.

I never saw the kid mowing again, fortunately. But a couple of months later a rescue vehicle and police cars were all over the lawn next-door. The mother of the child was being taken out on a stretcher. She had overdosed in the bathtub. They had found her too late. Within weeks the house stood empty again.

Haunt

I haunt the world like
a mangy dog broken leash
shady guy in old raincoat,
I skim the coast not
in frolicsome summer
but in off-season
poking snout into alleyways,
I scour midnight streets
when good folk should be in bed,
melting locks with time
to dig up traces of living,
then I'll spread the news about
the shadowed side of life.

Garden

Along the ocean coast, sand limits the growth of much flora. On the Bay the soil lies rich right up to the water line, so grasses, plants, and even tall trees thrive. Throughout the town you can see mixed hardwoods and conifers—sycamore, cedar, willow, spruce. Holly bushes often develop into trees.

We wanted to build our house facing east toward the Bay. We pushed it into the pine woods without having to take any down, so we were surrounded by green all year. The garden in front of us would get direct sun most of the day. We also wanted to use plants local to the region and limit any lawn to mow.

We laid out a curving pebbled path that ended in a sizable gray rock. To the Chinese this symbolized mountains. Pink and yellow moonbeam coreopsis soon billowed along the path. Even though near water, we sank a pond to get full effect; stocked with fat koy, gold and silver and blue-striped.

Then we planted a row of low gushing fountain grass in front of taller swaying feather grass; with two facing rows of bayberry hedge; Russian sage and a row of butterfly bushes, which when ripe hung down what looked like handfuls of tiny grapes.

Patches of gold brown-eyed susans, white daisies, purple cone flowers; a dogwood spotted here, cherry tree there amidst the garden.

Things even had color in autumn: michaelmas daisies' dark blue, red viburnums and winterberries, and sedum wore rouge. Blood grass truly lived up to its name in that season.

Bare areas in the shade of the pines we covered with English ivy or juniper rug or moss. We left an uncut buffer between our house and the house closest to us. Soon morning glory and trumpet flower vines proliferated; honeysuckle and multiflora added sweet aromas.

With bird feeders and bird houses, window boxes jammed with annuals like pansies, petunias, marigolds, we achieved our Swiss chalet effect; sometimes not knowing whether we were in or out of the house.

Time-Warp

It's what I had heard about
what I had hoped for,
last night's storm had savaged
the dunes though reinforced by
brown veins of frozen seagrass
resembling Snow White's seven
or Henrik Hudson's crew;
I approached a collapsed dune
to glimpse an ancient wooden keel,
perhaps in the interior
a chest—then out came tumbling
umbrellas, blankets, beach chairs—
summer again!

Modern Sailors

One summer two couples came to visit us to sail, towing their boats on trailers; one couple, then the following month the other. Though one was from New England, the other from the deep South, they were remarkably similar underneath. I had gotten to know the men better through business dealings over the years. However, each wife played an essential role in her husband's life.

Robert was a very unique individual. You would think a breakdown in college and later alcoholism might limit him. But he recovered to race motorcycles, work on a tug, and take first a psych then a library degree. He even found time to raise a huge garden. A short slim man who seldom looked directly at you; he often paused, spoke softly, revealed a depth of knowledge and a dry sense of humor.

It was an education to watch him and Jean ready their boat: he slow, deliberate; she overly energetic and always amiable, her more than generous breasts bouncing out of her t-shirt which read "New Hampshire: Live Free or Die!" If she overdid things, all it took was Robert's quiet but sharp command to get her in line. His precise movements and her ebullience dovetailed to put that boat neatly in the water.

I only noticed the parallels to Fielding and Nina as time went on. Fielding was a big man with a slow drawl; but ideas jumping like sparks. He too had done many things in his life: went to college for architecture, changed to history where he worked on a PhD till he found it involved too much cow-towing. He then became an ordained Methodist minister before also putting that behind him . He had built his own house, restored the car they drove, and had put together from scratch the sailboat they were now rigging.

Nina became a librarian to make ends meet while they raised their three boys. There had been talk in the past of possible wife-beating. I sincerely doubted it. At a restaurant after the sail, Nina cut in on Fielding's lengthy description of a past sailing incident: "Dear, you talk too much trash; and lay off that mayo, it's not good for your cholesterol." Fielding gave a broad smile and stroked his wife's shoulder tenderly.

Old Man's Reverie

The weight of life falls
so heavily on my
shoulders this morning,
knapsack filled with dark memories
mixed with flickers of light;
ironies around
the neck like a garrotte,
what should have been done
what should not—who knows
who cares, it wasn't;
on the distant shore
sun is still picking
out certain trees.

Extermination

(A letter from a friend)

I heard you were putting together a book about the Bay. Although I live a bit up the coast, I'm sure things happen here similar to where you are. So I send this along, for what it's worth.

My wife claims we live on the largest anthill in America. I can't fully agree with her. What with being close to the water and the inherent dampness, it draws ants naturally. Needless to say we have to hire an exterminator. Over the first year we hired one after another.

I'll never forget the first agent who arrived to sign us up. A very pretty girl, rosy complexion, short curls framing her face. But the skirt she was wearing—if I can even call it that—came way up on her thigh. I know it's the style but this girl tended to put on weight. Seemed as if she was oozing out of that skirt momentarily, and everything else she was barely wearing. Wife and I exchanged glances. I signed up, however. Guess she took advantage of me.

The next ex-pert--let me call them that since they failed to curtail the ants—was an elf of a man. He was older and slow-going , but I thought he had the expertise. Turned out he did little but stand by the door and talk about the Bay; its dawns, sunsets, winter freezes, hot spells, boat wrecks, etc. All, I must admit, interesting but where were the results of extermination?

A woman appeared next; short hair, piercings all over. Seems she was an impersonator. Did a hell of an Elvis, I must admit. Talked about her club gigs, how much she made moonlighting. I wondered, if she was so good, why she didn't do it full time? Last service she gave us, she was thinking about a sex change operation.

Months had gone by. We were tired out by now. The ants were having daily stadium jamborees. A guy arrives. I just groaned inside. A shaved head, bandanna, tattoos. Bragged about all his motorcycle racing. But by God, he cured the place of ants! He knew his business. Trick was to find the nests outside, spray all around the house, even down the driveway.

Now we don't have to hold our breath every morning when we see those crisscrossing ant trails over the kitchen counters and down the cupboard doors. Seems like a minor thing in the strife of life, but it now gives us peace of mind.

Along the Patchwork Coast

Clean smooth sky, blues and whites
applied in wide sweeps.
Loud speedboat passes
shaped like chaise longue
sitting high on water.
On lowered window shade
a stain resembling Spain,
squashed fly the capital.
Marina for sale,
ghosts of boats bobbing
not even dock left,
sign remains: RHONDA'S LIPS
only gulls remember.

From a Daybook – I

I don't shoot geese over the marshes. I don't pull jeweled bass from the sea. I don't drive a power boat. I'm a proud landlubber, a watcher. Perhaps I observe more closely the flora and fauna along the fringes of the Bay.

The tone of weekly mornings is different from weekend ones in this fishing village. During the week the early day is filled with sounds of screeching, metal slamming, motors starting. Everyone is involved: mothers cooking, children going to school, fathers launching. A weekend morning really begins the night before. It is the notes of a trumpet from a boat party, a last couple of laughs, a few phrases of farewell.

Reluctantly went to Rotary Club meeting in Historical Society building through beautiful green park on river. Geese grazing, ducks floating near sandy bank. Scene of many boats on river nearly dissuaded me from going in. Avoided an open bar to find a pianist playing background music in corner. Sat on piano bench with him to discover he was from NYC. Knew Coltrane, Adderley, Mulligan. Made my day.

Fourth of July, boats have come up river at dusk for the festivities. Hundreds of them hover, their red running lights revealing just their port sides. Feeling mid-river too, we stand at end of the pier watching the fireworks. Bugs pour to death on the bug lights, babies cry, kids jump at each new explosion. We older ones now and then can't hold back gasps at the brilliance. Party over, boats head down river, now only green lights against the dark.

A serendipity drive along the Bay found us in a swank retirement village.
No pick-up trucks, t-shirts, even obesity. Men in Bermudas, women in
sun dresses played shuffleboard or badminton. Sipping lemonades in
a gazebo. Raked sand and beach umbrellas. Immaculate little cottages
dotted the Bay. No plastic over windows, unfinished additions, not one
rusting fridge in the yard.

Autumn. I watch the loblolly trees cry down rain on the window panes
of this café. The place symbolizes the thirties when our grandparents
slopped around the floor cheek to cheek in their hot youth. Juke box,
player piano, crank phone on the wall, posters of the newest DeSotos
and Hudsons and Studes. The dark paneled walls make the place cool in
summer, dank in autumn, even the beer in this mug seems musty.

Holton's Restaurant has best seafood in area. We sat on second floor
porch overlooking main street and Bay. Sitting behind us group of
women who (it appears) took their daughters to lunch; lot of giggling
and exchanging of wrapped gifts. Festive air. Wife had bass, our friend
ordered crabs, I tried fried oysters. All delicious. Open-air market below
us has farmers speaking Italian, Thais selling oriental vegetables.

Interesting used bookstore cum antique shop. Walking in you feel you're
in owners' living room. There they sit, but everything for sale. Ceiling to
floor books in every room on three floors. Fitting that I found a trove
of Thoreaus, bought two. On way out door, struck up conversation with
very old man sitting on stoop who turned out to be retired sea captain.
Grizzled face and carved cane. Tale of voyage to Patagonia made me late
for dinner.

Historic tour day. Our town boasts some lovely 18th century homes. Willamette House has a gigantic central chimney. Tompkins House hides a secret staircase from attic to cellar. Present owners of Titus House greeted us in Revolutionary clothes, even offering cider and ginger snaps. Our cackling tour guide led us across street like a herd of chickens—not even checking as cars screeched to a stop.

Water is always in the background. It is our natural habitat. It is our ancestor. It is a path; adventure in its length. Then open sea becomes the universe. Death lies in its depths, or hidden life. Across a span of water a new language may wait. The Bay always lurks; disguised by current during day, detected by a sound at night like rumbling or chanting. Along its banks all peoples have gathered, played, grown and passed, making way for each new generation. Eternal lights overhead are recast in water. The better to see into ourselves.

Thyme by Moonlight

Picking thyme by moonlight
plants flavor our food
favor our destiny
color imaginings
create rhythms which drive us,
pansies become lips
petunias trumpets;
picking thyme by moonlight
your face changes to silver,
in water your face is the moon
that light make coolness, softness,
stream sweeping round a headland
currents spreading you into ocean.

S. S. Minnow

Summers when I was a boy, I liked to wander around the docks of a little shore town. I collected worthless junk, but my imagination turned nothing into something. A couple of bolts, strip of leather, staves from a broken barrel became a submarine or a bomb. I still love the smell of diesel and tar. Maybe I get that from those youthful times.

I guess I picked up those ideas originally when I visited my cousin in the city for a weekend. He lived near a train yard where discarded detritus lay all over. We imagined we could make a bomb to create a major derailment; violence a large part of our boys' fantasy world. Then we went back to his house to swap baseball cards.

I always preferred the Bay to the ocean. On an ocean beach all you saw were people sun-tanning, picnicking, maybe playing volleyball—boring. I was always wondering what I could see on the horizon or just beyond the harbor. No wonder those childhood feelings rang bells when as a college student I read The Last Puritan or South Wind.

My sole thrill at the beach was when a whale washed up. It was monumental. Some kids had worked their way up on top by means of its rear fin and wobbly were pacing its length. That was before it started to stink and the authorities arrived to rope off the area and cut up the carcass with chain saws. I had a recurring nightmare: as I walked by, the eye flapped open and the sand beneath the whale trembled as he whispered, Help me—Give me a push!

Now in our town there is a boat washed up. It's been there quite a while. Honeysuckle grows through its exposed ribs and an ironic sign hangs on its stern: S.S. Minnow. Of course you think of Gilligan's Island. I also think of Robinson Crusoe and Treasure Island. I wonder, as it slowly dissolves into the landscape, what kind of cargo, if any, it ever carried of worth. It's enough to set you imagining.

Muted

I learned to see tones in your
Scotland and in subtleties
of black and white photos;
now in the local marsh
among ten types of brown
and a score of grays
as our dory barely moves
through cattails and sawgrass
I discern what you
are softly saying;
our travels and stay-at-homes
define us, sharpen
what we really mean and feel.

Art of The Bay

The most ancient Asian scroll paintings have bodies of water in them. Misty mountains climb into the sky, with a hint of ocean beyond, a fisherman poling on a lake, a gushing waterfall on a braided river.

Through the centuries flashes of the Nile are glimpsed in Egyptian frescoes or flying fish on Greek pottery. After all, towns carried on trade and ports encouraged trade, especially foreign, as much as overland routes, if not more.

The Dutch realist painters like Rembrandt made water traffic with its types of vessels, piers, docks, wharves an inherent part of the scenes of life.

The French Impressionists—see Van Gogh's "Bank of the Rhone," Sisley's "Boats on the Seine," Monet's "Bridge at Argenteuil"— utilized brilliant colors almost blinding the viewer as sunlight off the water can do.

Like Van Gogh coming from Holland to France, Turner with his tonal explosions was the bridge to English artists like Constable, who captured more peaceful river and lake scenes, cattle serenely ankle-wading. Whistler would come later with works like his "Nocturne in Blue and Silver."

The eastern coast of the United States spawned painters like John Marin and Albert Ryder. Being so poor, Ryder panted on cheap wood which now is starting to disintegrate. Winslow Homer loved to paint boulders and crashing waves, overcast skies, and fishermen caught in heavy weather; he even went to England for a while to gather further scenes and techniques.

Artists lurk everywhere by the sea. Gauguin explored South Sea life; in the West Indies Larry Gluck created thousands of lithographs, from boats ready to sail to dark winding seafront alleys. Our Bay can be rough in storm and winter weather; ships still search out safe harbor up the rivers and in the estuaries. The full brunt of a hurricane is rare around here.

Photos we take of families at the beach are now too numerous to count. Man came from the sea and continually wishes to get back. Beachfront is so populous that it takes diligent searching to find a tranquil location on the coast; now a costly investment too.

Fireworks All Weekend

Night fireworks reveal
in a field grinning pre-teens.
Fireworks above rock band
display danse macabre.
Fireworks on the Bay
disclose in a boat
less than clothes.
Fireworks middle of a street
stop short trooper's cruiser.
Flash of fireworks sporadic,
crackle and concussion
like distant battle
through the Fourth.

A Moonlit Sail

The ad in the local paper sounded unique: With your special other let the wind and moonlight caress your fantasies. Exquisite wine and cheese, conversation and romance on an authentic Bay "Clipper."

The crowd was quite mixed as we gathered at the pier. Certainly not all lovers—some families, even kids. Oh well, I guess everybody is entitled. We clambered aboard and found a cozy seat on a hatch. The available chairs were taken. We bought tickets from a choice of three dapper young men in pseudo sailor uniforms who were roaming the deck.

Out of the harbor we went, by engine power. I guess they had to wait till open Bay to get that huge sail up. I was beginning to want to clink wine glasses with my "special other." I hoped they had brie for it was her favorite.

Glasses were being handed out. I guess plastic was best because real glass could easily slip from a hand on a pitching deck. The pseudo sailors thrust magnums of wine at our out held glasses—nice choice, white or red. My wife and I looked at each other, tasting mediocre wine at best.

Here came the cheese on tilting trays. Paws snatched left and right. Why did we decide the stern would be the most romantic? We were the last served—some multicolored toothpicks, a few fragments of cheese, looked like cheddar.

Not wishing to break what was left of the mood, I was about to whisper a little something into my wife's ear when the loud-speaker announced: For nearly a week ,unfortunately, it seems there has not been a bit of wind again tonight. We cannot raise the sail, but we do not want to disappoint you. So we shall motor fully around the harbor to give you a pleasurable excursion.

I was fuming, my wife shrugged. Then I caught the eye of a chipper old lady. She leaned toward us: Isn't this wonderful! My grandson and I are from Abilene. We've never been east before, in all my years. His parents decided to stay on shore in the motel to watch TV. But I wouldn't have missed this for anything. The Bay is so beautiful!

Even her little Ricky seemed to be enjoying himself. Stiffly my wife and I returned her broad smile. It was a sincere one. I looked around, squeezed my wife's hand; the moonlight on the water was truly magnificent.

Between 3 And 4 A. M.

A woman's voice slashes
through darkness, rising
from the lower depths.
Mumbled and meandering,
it moves along the dock
then through narrow streets
of this harbor town.
Is she drunk?
Is she angry?
Is she insane?
After a torturous time of
wondering, the voice ceases as if
a banshee had given warning.

Fruits of Summer

Plump fruit fills summer. Fruits hanging from trees, cached in crotches of branches, stuffed in thickets like lost beach balls; fruits on torrid roofs or along smoldering highways. Hang out any hot window to see green carpets, green tapestries, a teal sky against which are embossed all kinds of fruit. Any man-made things are colored: awnings, umbrellas, signs, ships. People walk bedecked in oranges and grapes and grapefruits. Nature-made things too boast hues: flowers and birds, trees and bushes, plants and shrubs.

People in cars, on bikes, on skates, on jogging legs—all painted in their own stripes. On the beach heaps of bodies in varied shades of pinks and tans and golds. Curvaceous women, muscle-ridden men, children in drooping shorts strut their stuff. Fruits of dogs roll and leap and scratch and twitch. Bright shiny fruits are pulled from the Bay, as fruits fly over in planes and copters and hang-gliders. On the sky are scrawled carts of watermelons, maidens in bonnets amid strawberry fields, under palms bathing suits munching guavas, mangos, papayas. The world tingles with energy!

June is low simmer, July a baking, August abroil. While in the kitchen I in garish apron—painted wares in French: "fromage, beurre, moutard, lait"—a banner wrapped tight, toss items like the ultimate juggler. Extravaganza of omelet (think of color!): mushrooms, cheeses, tomatoes, black olives, red peppers, purple onions. Oatmeal: raisins, bananas, blackberries, blueberries, cherries, peaches. Or a salad: avocados, celery, green olives, carrots, orange peppers, cucumbers, water chestnuts, bamboo shoots, table setting of lettuce.

Music on the beach, on shadowed porches, among groves, in clubs at night, by star-rimmed Bay water. I sniff sod and leaf and flesh, burger, salt and heat. Earth and Bay open their jeweled cornucopia.

Visit From Gustav

No snow on the trees
just the thought of it,
stars diced ice in the water.
Ocean a gray line
a sand-colored parallel line,
Gustav stood with a gift
in each nervous hand.
As a young man he had to
decide to send his mother
to an asylum.
He had worked his entire life
so that people could not say
he came from a deprived home.

Parrothead

Growing to manhood Frank Russo had two assets going for him. He could weld anything of metal. He could have worked in a garage, built high rises, become a sculptor. Instead he decided to teach shop in high school. Each year the students grew more rowdy and defiant. He had had to make too many compromises with the administration. He had been disgraced too often. He thought his temper was warranted.

After his first marriage had failed—he didn't know why his wife had left him before he had time to leave her —he didn't know why his son never talked to him. He moved to Graysheep Bay. There things seemed to turn around. He bought a couple houses, fixed them up, and became a slumlord. He invested in a 36 –ft cabin cruiser. When he married a pleasant, plump woman who owned her own cleaning service, he thought he had found gold. They even mortgaged a house in Florida to live during the winter months.

But the story gets ahead of us. Let's go back a few years. Frank Russo's other asset was that he resembled Ernest Hemingway.

At least he thought so. And other people had remarked about it. When his beard started to gray, he thought one day he could do something special with this gift. He had fallen in love with living on the Bay. He saw his boat as a beautiful and powerful work of art. He was taken by the sunrises and sunsets, the rolling in and out of the tides. He started to collect Jimmy Buffet albums and wear French sailor shirts.

Then he heard about the Ernest Hemingway look alike contest held each year in Key West. He would go there to win a little money, but more importantly—fame.

When he arrived for the big contest night in Dirty Harry's Bar, he couldn't believe the scene. The place was jammed and noisy. Everything was tropical—from the shirts to the décor. Waiters wore parrot heads, waitresses hula skirts. Women wore wet t-shirts and sarongs, leis and much less. However, it was the men who staggered him. Every male in the place had a beard.

Frank paid to enter the contest (a considerable sum), scanned the crowd and grinned. Many of the men looked nothing like all the photos of Hemingway he had collected over the years.

Then it got serious. All contestants were asked to stand along the bar, facing three judges who slowly worked their way down the line. Frank thought the rogues gallery were phonies. Again he thought they looked nothing like his macho Papa with whom he could have been a twin.

They passed on and made their judgments. He didn't even place! The winner sort of resembled Hem but not really. Frank broke through the crowd and cornered
the head judge.

"Hey, why didn't I even place?" His eyes were popping—the months of anticipation, the long trip, the money.

"Say, friend, this is an honest objective contest. You have a pretty similar beard. But Hemingway was over six feet tall. What are you—maybe five foot seven?"

Out of Season

Dawn light through marshgrass
makes smoke mixing with
haze on the horizon,
sea the blue-gray tone
of a shot-gun barrel.
I'm coming to an end up north,
you'd think this beauty
would sustain me, but
in a mere few months
duck-hunting begins.
Each sailboat beneath each cliff
its canvas taut and on course,
the puff of a dream.

Bay Towns

Over the years each town has developed its own character. Sometimes the personality changed, but it became strongly imprinted on the town.

Pierretown took on a certain elegance. It certainly wasn't easy to do, backed up between the coast and Route #10 which grew busier and busier each decade. It wisely conserved many of the older houses. It turned a fortress of a stone nunnery into an office complex. It built an art center, a history museum, and an outdoor theater right along the shore. The town fathers even put in a nature boardwalk which snaked its way through the marsh in the inlet. A preserved 18th century lighthouse was the topping on the cake.

Willowville went artsy-craftsy. It has only one street—long and narrow. Along this artery sprung up in addition to the arts a wide variety of shops: a bakery, a bookstore, ice cream place, tea house, a bait & tackle shop, local newspaper office. An ex 5 & 10 became an antique cooperative; two floors of alcoves holding mostly Americana. The town also boasted a direct tie to the water with the development of a museum documenting the Bay's history: boats, nets, sails, decoys, and many photos of watermen and the town in earlier times.

Our town went in a different direction. It pulled inwards to become a quiet family haven; although at times some members of the family could act up. We rejected all retail stores, even ripped up the tanks of an old gas station. We grew to respect the green potential around us. Our beaches, though small, are clean; we offer free vehicle parking and a boat dock, even a park for daytime recreation.

Some people rave about the New England and Mid-Atlantic shores. But getting there in better months takes long lines of cars—then hours getting home. While you're there, compete for room on the beach or in a restaurant.

You can get even more exotic about the lure of beaches and dream about, say, Ireland. In the dead middle of summer if it gets into the sixties, that's hot to the Irish. They sit on the sand shivering then go home bragging about their tan, which is just a slight reddishness like they had rubbed too much with a towel.

Or the Riviera—ever been there? I have. The beach is hell to sit or walk on, composed of stones—not the fine sand we take for granted here.

Swamp Walk

We trace a narrow boardwalk
winding over marshland
like gods hovering
in air to cast a spell.
Yet the spell is upon us
with gems of hummingbirds
and bursting goldenrod.
Distant once-a-day train
wah-wahs and rasps along
its rusty rails. Scat points out
beasts having been here at night,
but we imagine lost
lovers in the sun.

Tides

I – Approach

As we leave the traffic we can also feel the terrain narrow. Practically all
the land is turning to sand. Without dark glasses the world would burn
up. But amazingly the shore breeze dissipates direct heat. Only glare
persists. Our auto follows the curl of land into the sea. Deeper, deeper,
passed sand dunes now like bastions. Strange little houses brown-shin-
gled and seeming delicate. How could they withstand the gales we know
must blow out of the heart of the sea. Imagine this scene in winter.
Sky blows black, wind scours cement, lights die out of houses. In rain
all would float away; or return to undersea landscape. Now in summer,
cyclone fences stand foolish as sand sifts through them. We pass an
occasional bicycle. The waterline hides, but we hope humans possess the
beach. Now and then a rowboat, like a dab of paint on the Bay to which
the painter returned. Our invisible driveway of sand is on the left beyond
the brace of maiboxes. Only sawgrass waves in the yard and discarded
barnacles. The toughened house patiently waits to be patted; to be opened
to the light.

II – Self-Portrait

She was surfacing out of sleep. The sunlight touched her shoulder. She
lay there listening. Sounds told her that breakfast was almost over. Noises
on the back porch said that some were on their way to the beach. She
got out of bed wearing pajama bottoms and sat at her vanity in front of
the mirror. Morning light told the truth. Her breasts were full and high;
a man would never mistake them for pillows that strangled. She tried a
rhinestone choker; to a man it would look restraining. She tried a gold
locket that hung silent. A dab of perfume brought her senses to life.
Coming in for lunch she changed out of her bathing suit. Her buttocks
seemed bronze in the light. The sea, the earth, something was changing,
rarified. At dusk she was naked by the window. The sand dunes were

naked. The light painted shadows on her body. From a distance he would see only a stroke of color against the sand. Here she was multi-dimensional. The shadows enlarged her body.

III – Visitors

Now when the phone rings it is always joy. At each ring excitement grows, like angels ringing down incense. Each tinkle is a little dance in the soul; despite the coldness of the room. In the shadows the anticipation cools my brow. Yes, the conversation is innocent. Sometimes just silence of listening, longing; an old friend chatting. But a secret history hides under words; amid family cross-words, the chess moves. Beneath light conversation your essence waits. In leisure among them I read your letters; here you may say anything. How you desire, how we want each other. Our desire has been lengthy, circuitous, but it still lives. You describe acts which make me cough. I am sure my face burns, thank god, underneath the make-up of sunburn. I rise, to the kitchen for iced tea, lean against the sink. Outside into the backyard of sand and silence. On a wooden bench in the shadow of the house eaves, I remember so much. Intensity is so eternal and set in my inmost parts. Your passing by on the street is like a tree; full-blooming branches stirred by summer breezes. If I could touch you; but your thought touches me more deeply. The tension has become part of living. Do we both understand that. Do we accept.

IV – Diving

He dives; it is what he has planned. He has found solitude, rowed out into the Bay. A quiet day, boat bobbing slightly. He feels his legs stretched out against the wood. The sunlight covers his upper body. Now he is bathed in salty drops of warmth. Soon the cool underworld. He pulls off his shorts, experiences the shock of ultimate nakedness. Stands a moment, as if defying the pedantic shoreline. He dives, feels the shock of cold liquid weight. Down, down he goes; into a green world where light is spectral. Stretches arms, kicks legs, inhales once again. He sees her. She is waiting for him; a green creature, all faces. Her breasts are full and confident. They point toward him like twin knives. Touching their coolness he finds perfection, not unlike the cliché of living marble, he ponders. Their eternal kiss begins. As tongues entwine he seems to feel her inhale him; begins to feel her engorge him. One stray thought flutters his closing eyes; how far to the surface, how far away he is.

V – Shoreline

Why is the sky so high, the clouds so distant? The only cry of wildlife the harshness of the seagull. Sun has contracted to a burning eye. Wind rasps through sea plants on the beach. Wind blows onto the blanket like a roll of the dice. I look at the old man's face. If you work through grizzle, splotches, wrinkles, the power is still there. Estimating the moment, the mood is difficult. He sits in pants which show pale ankles. My dress billows as I sit. This bright print brings needed flowers to this severe setting. Under the straw hat fringes of his hair are alive in the breeze. The young people without exception are dark, dark all over with little to hide. And yet genitals are all to them. The unabridged books, the unguarded song. Touch of hands on bodies, postures that provoke and permit. They are all like a foreign place. Have I grown so far from them? Yet retain the residue of desires, desires I refine through distance, distances of space and indirectness. I yearn for more, but is it at base just the touch of a body which knows mine. Can it be so simple and so elusive. The beach should tell me all I need to know. I have become a blind sibyl, reading tea leaves, palms, eyelids. Still feeling more than I know.

Not Go Back

I can not go back
to where we were queen
and king of the mountain,
the meadow, the woodland,
where we were higher
than sleeping dawn clouds.
Though things continue to change
let politics, sports
science have their ways,
I will stay by the Bay
where things flow eternally
and though surface shifts,
the essentials remain.

Furnishings

What furnishings go well with the Bay? No lobster trap for a coffee table, no carved wooden seagulls above the fireplace, no whale harpoon over the hall door; no brass ship's bell nor shells in a glass lamp.

These days it's all persons for themselves. There is no right décor; it is what you personally like and feel comfortable with.

Certainly our elephant table. Its top is inlaid with mosaics of ivory. Tiny ivory beads trace the circular edge. Replicas of elephant heads in ivory make up the three legs which uniquely support it. It has traveled over a lot of water to get here from India.

The rectangular slab of pink marble sitting on four brass legs came all the way from Carrara.

Likewise the three Chinese lamps traveled a long distance. One is simply a large blue vase; but the vase is the deepest blue, the color of unpolluted ocean. The other is black with white chrysanthemums dotting it. And the third, the most joyful to me, is a scene in yellows and greens and reds of people at a feast, all in motion.

Wicker and rattan chairs capture that West Indian flavor of lightness blended with durability.

A staunch Amish desk, being handmade, gives a certain quiet beauty, its golden finish glowing in late afternoon sunlight.

An ornately carved library chair with pillows embroidered in sea scenes; the leering gargoyles on the end of each chair arm give a laugh to a very dark veneer.

A brass Turkish oil lamp hanging in the hallway must have swung in ships plying the Mediterranean coast all the way from Byzantium to Gibraltar.

Out of Water

On rainy days slow
autos alter into
dark vessels at sea,
their running lights and
mournful echoings of
horns in the constant down-
pour warn of night passings;
out of fire and air
sunlight is for living, but
water from above, below,
raises the gray dead out of
shipwreck sleep or moldy clay,
a bare moment to glimpse.

On the Bay

Slats of sunlight lay on his chest. The room looked white, even the dust on the floor looked clean. He got out of the chair. He was wearing a t-shirt and shorts.

He pushed open the screen door and walked onto the porch. The mug of coffee was still hot in his hands. He sipped and looked up the arrow of a street. He swung his head in the other direction. The Bay was three blocks away where he could just make out the white caps.

He walked through the village to the dock where his rowboat was dipping in the wakes of motorboats. He bought bait and rowed to the middle of the Bay. He stuck the clam on the hook and let the line sink.

When the sinker hit bottom, he got a better sense of the Bay. The currents pulled at the line but he knew when a fish hit. He eased out the line then tugged it. When the fish was caught, he reeled it in.

It was a sea robin. Its mouth was not torn. He held it with one hand and eased out the hook with the other. He looked at its unfocused eye then dropped it back in.

The sun did not penetrate his head. The next time he caught a porgy of good size. He rowed in, taking long strokes with the oars, trying to pull them in fluid unison. He felt his back muscles ripple.

He sat on the steps and gutted the fish. Two large cats stalked through the yard. He sliced the meat cleanly away from the back bone. He put the fish on the ground and moved away. The cats edged up to the fish and glanced around. Hunching, they ripped off little chunks and chewed.

He held the skeleton and peered at it. The bones were in perfect symmetry. He put the skeleton on top of the tool shed where tomorrow it would be bleached bright white.

It was low tide as he walked along the gray strip of sand that was usually covered by water. A little raking with fingers turned up a clam. He squatted and studied the other shells and tiny pools of water. With one finger he pushed a hole into the sand. It was easy to find a sand crab which he let tickle his finger.

He collected two dozen clams which were there for the taking. He cooked the clams for dinner, eating them with garlic butter and French bread. He drank cheap burgundy from a jelly glass making a red ring on the white wooden tabletop.

At dusk he walked along the beach. He picked up a piece of driftwood that looked like a carver had turned it with a knife. He looked into the lighted windows of the houses on the beach. The people inside resembled paintings. He was glad to be outside.

He passed a couple under a blanket. He was close enough to hear them groan. He walked home and took a steaming shower.

The next morning someone knocked on the door. It was his wife. "Tom, are you down here again?" she asked. She was slender and always stylishly dressed.

"I like it here," he answered.

"Why do you want to be alone so much?" Paula asked.

"It's quiet."

"This is the fourth weekend in a row. You'll be getting a three-week vacation in August." She lit a cigarette.

"I worked hard to buy this house," Tom said. "I'm going to retire here one day."

"But what will the children say?"

"They've got to live their own lives."

She sat down at the kitchen table and tossed her handbag on it. "The radio says there's going to be a storm."

"I'm going to take a bike ride," Tom said. "Want to come?"

She did not answer. The road was flat and straight so he pedaled hard. In twenty minutes he made it to the tip of the peninsula. He walked around the base of the lighthouse which had stood there since 1884. They still worked the light at night. A strong wind was blowing over the large rocks and the sky was gray.

When he got back to the house, he was winded. Paula was wearing a bathing suit. "I went to the beach but it was too cold.," she said.

"I'll go to the deli and buy some things," he said.

It began to rain as he walked two blocks to the store which wasn't crowded.
Food was jammed onto shelves. He bought a six-pack of beer, a small eye roast, a bottle of milk, and some razor blades.

When he got back she said,"I want to talk some more."

"I'll listen,"Tom said putting the roast into the oven.

"What's happening to you?"she asked.

Slowly he answered, "You've always been so sure of yourself. You make the confusion then clean it up. You can do anything."

She didn't answer but lit another cigarette. He looked out the window where there was water now running in the street. "It's going to be a big blow," he said. They sat and listened to the wind rattling the house.

Later he went out to the street to check his car. The water was up to the hubcaps. On his way back to the house two rats scurried from under the porch. A wooden rocking chair was shifting on the lawn.

Paula was standing in the kitchen. "I'm scared, Tom."

"It'll be a storm not a hurricane," he said.

"How can you be so sure?"

"I'm not."

"I want to call the children."

"Go ahead," he said checking the roast.

Her eyes looked very round to him. He moved to her and put his hand on her shoulder. As she leaned into him, he put his arms around her.

"Are we going to die?" she smiled wanly.

"One day."

"I don't know what's going on inside of you," she said.

"You don't listen. I'm simple."

"And stubborn."

"And worked around."

The house shook. "I'm scared. I need you." She sounded like a stranger to him.

They lay in bed listening and dozing. Soon he slept and dreamed that his white suit was on the bed. He put it on with a red tie. He drove across the Bay bridge to the town that had liquor and music. He went to several bars. Sitting at the bar he drank beer. He talked to the bartender and to people near him.

At one bar he talked to a girl. He liked her looks. They danced and he liked what she said. They went to two more bars together. Then she went home with him. All of the windows were open in the car. When he stopped for a light, the air was warm. When the car was moving, the breeze was cold.

They stood on the porch of his house. They saw the lights across the Bay where they had been. Holding hands they went inside where he turned on the radio till he found soft music. They lay on the bed and kissed. Then they undressed and made love.

Later the radio was still playing softly. They were still holding hands which were entwined like a piece of sculpture. He could feel her pulse. He suddenly realized that she looked like his wife. He kissed her eyelids till she woke.

But he was waking and Paula was next to him in the soft morning light. The storm was over and the house was sound. They had slept late. Finally they got up and went outside.

The Bay seemed the same until they took a walk. They closely studied sections of soil that had been washed away. A pier stood out of the water at high tide. The shoreline had changed a lot. But the sky was bright.

Into the Wooden Bowl

As I shred the lettuce
autumn leaves are plummeting,
tomatoes giant-size
versions of berries
on the viburnum bush,
thin slices of yellow pepper
while thin slices of late
afternoon sun lie
on the pine-planked floor,
for dessert I decide
we shall have bluest berries
glancing at the Bay
below the kitchen window.

Especially Autumn

I think you appreciate the world more in autumn. You feel a tingle of some change coming; it might be difficult. So now becomes all important to enjoy. You inhale deeply; autumn air is clear and smells like pure oxygen. Unlike summer air which is seductive as honey; it smells of a dozen scenes—sea, sand, skin, sex. Summer massages you with oils; fall vigorously raps you on the back to get going.

Autumn air has eternity in it. And the end too. But if you believe Einstein, since the universe is curved, when you come to an end it's the beginning of something else.

As you get up on an autumn morning, things are not summer soft and warm and sensual. They are sharp, compelling and sensuous. The Bay sparkles, glimmers, gleams. The tide—so high it is going to spill the bucket—rushes in and out. A crow's early morning caw can split the air, so you wake stark upright wondering what is dream or not. At night a couple people whispering at the foot of the hill can be heard uptown. My vision even seems to clear up in the fall; no guarding against the July sweat seeping into eyes.

I know for sure autumn is here as I sit on the deck. In the garden sedum has turned pink, the michaelmas are a bright royal purple and the bloodgrass lives up to its red description. Who says an autumn green is not colorful; Queen Anne's lace adds the dabs of white, and goldenrod the yellow. I learned to discern muted colors in the Scottish highlands. A first glance gives you an impression that the landscape is just brown. Closer examination—close and patient—reveals another palette, another plane or universe of shades

I'm ready for painting or window-washing; I'd prefer a walk along the shore.

Extended

He stutters here, there,
moths of memories
fluttering round his ears.
A green or purple
sunrise?—he's seen them all.
From the black toenail
to the wen on his skull
he's become an extension
of deviations.
In the neverending
current he can sink
softly into sand
or take final bearings.

The Shore

Scientific writing about the sea is legion: treatises, pamphlets, studies, histories; Thoreau's *Cape Cod* or Beston's *Outermost House* a tiny sampling. Since poets for the most part focus on nature, manifestations of water are a major theme.

I've always been especially fond of Edgar Allan Poe's *The Gold Bug*. Somewhere on an island off the Carolinas a man and his servant search for a treasure; if they drop a tiny gold piece in shape of a bug through the eye socket of a skull propped in a tree, they will discover a fabulous cache.

Whaling was a major industry for 19th century America. Herman Melville delineated that life in *Moby Dick*; he was a master author of the sea with other books like *Omoo, Typee, White Jacket.* The sea is part of the American lifeblood; fishing and trading by water, next to farming, were major ways to make a living.

Nathaniel Hawthorne seldom wrote about the sea in his novels; yet you can sense Salem's impending fog and odor of brine behind him. As a miniaturist his short stories and sketches, like *Foot-prints on the Sea-shore*, take place on the beach.
Jack London, author of *The Sea Wolf*, had actually been a fisherman on the California coast and owned a magnificent sailing ship. Rudyard Kipling, although British, had married an American wife; his novel *Captains Courageous* came from having lived for years in Vermont.

Great American books have been written about the sea. Wandering through a bookshop we might happen upon:

John Barth, *The Floating Opera*
Peter Benchly, *Jaws*
Henry Beston, *The Outermost House*
Richard Henry Dana, *Two Years before the Mast*
Robert Finch, *Cape Cod Notebook*
Nathaniel Hawthorne, *Foot-prints on the Sea-shore*
Sterling Hayden, *Wanderer*

Ernest Hemingway, *The Old Man and the Sea*
Joseph Hergesheimer, *Java Head*
Sarah Orne Jewett, *Country of the Pointed Firs*
Rudyard Kipling, *Captains Courageous*
Anne Morrow Lindbergh, *Gift from the Sea*
Jack London, *The Sea Wolf*
Herman Melville, *Moby Dick*
James Michener, *Chesapeake*
Henry Miller, *The Colossus of Marousi*
Edgar Allan Poe, *The Gold Bug*
Wyman Richardson, *The House on Nauset Marsh*
May Sarton, *The House by the Sea*
John Steinbeck, *Cannery Row*
Robert Stone, *Outerbridge Reach*
Harriet Beecher Stowe, *The Pearl of Orr's Island*
William Styron, *Tidewater Tales*
Celia Thaxter, *Among the Isles of Shoals*
Henry Thoreau, *Cape Cod*
Henry Van Dyke, *Little Rivers*
Herman Wouk, *The Caine Mutiny*

In Situ

We are not summer people,
we don't measure mid-point
by July Four nor end
by Labor Day, shedding a tear
gearing up for work by rote.
We are a hand behind
the waving gingham curtain
we are eyes in trees,
we abide hot crowds
and noise as we do the tides
for we are the sands
slightly shifting but there,
our challenge sullen winter.

A Block Away

One street over from us is a little house for rent. It's the old story of greed. A quiet old lady with a heart condition but a solid pension lived there. Yet the landlord upped the rent beyond her budget. Then a nice young man moved in. He was away most of the week working at a nearby Navy yard. When he was home he mowed the grass and, being handy, fixed up the house. The landlord upped him—and suffered the rewards of hell.

A family moved in, but it turned out to be more of a clan. Neighbors told me people arrived and left all hours of the day and night. You would estimate three or four persons could live there at the most. But a dozen or more would be sitting out in good weather then all disappear inside till the next day. One day two little kids would be playing in the yard; next day three entirely different ones. Vehicles piled up in the driveway. Heavy metal was played loud; we could hear it easily on our block.

Things got no better. One four AM a woman came screaming out of the house, a man after her. He caught her in the middle of the street and began to beat her. A neighbor yelled that he was calling the cops. By the time the troopers arrived, the man had gone back into the house. The woman denied that anything had happened.

The neighborhood was seething. A garage had been broken into and its tools sold in the next town. The seller was recognized as living in the rental. Those tenants were even stealing lawnmower cans of gas from nearby houses for their cars. A committee went to the landlord who said he didn't give a damn as long as they paid the monthly rent.

A group of townsmen went to the house and stood in a line in the street. They told the family to leave or they would take the law into their own hands. That seemed to get the message across. But for spite a week after they were finally gone, there was vandalism all over town one night. No one could prove that outlaw family did it. We all wondered what the landlord had to pay to fix up that trashed house for the next poor sucker.

New in Town

The moon played with
the tides again last night.
I'm new to this town but
yesterday Singapore
with sweat beads pasted
to faces of buildings
as well as humans'.
Today Oslo , cold wind
cutting under the eyes
to form bruised pouches.
I pass an elegant house
to sniff a swath of garlic,
realizing possibilities.

Water Games

Perhaps the most personal expression in the arts, as well as the experience by a listener, is music. Really any sound can mean anything, depending on the individual ear. What is cacophony to some is white noise to others.

In any event some composers have created tones that mean something specific to them. Smetana was thinking about a river when he composed *The Moldau*; likewise Strauss with *The Blue Danube*. Lizst and Sibelius envisioned lakes with *Beside Lake Wallenstatdt* and *The Swans of Tuonela*. Schubert saw a trout in his *Quintet*. Ravel and Handel were dreaming in generality about bodies of liquid with their individual *Water Music*.

But the lion's share of major water works focuses on the ocean: Mendelssohn's *Hebrides Overture*, Debussy's *La Mer*, Vaughan-Williams' *Sea Symphony*, Rachmaninoff's *Isle of the Dead*, Richard Rogers' *Victory at Sea*. Without a title would you still be able to hear and see and feel (even taste) the ocean?

Water played key roles in man's life and development. It rained forty days and nights, then the flood allowed Noah's ark to rediscover the earth. The sea parted for the Israelites when they escaped from Egypt. A believer was baptized in the River Jordan; and today babies are still blessed with water at the beginning of their lives. A stormy day does not have to portend gloom; rainy fertility promises new growth.

People are drawn to the water for some explainable reasons but also by instinctual pulls. Certainly musicians have always heard the sounds of the sea: the many moods of the water, the varied voice of birds; the more prosaic sounds of motors on or off shore. Plus, all those sand-related Beach Boy songs or East Coast rock & rolling on the pier.

Conversation at a boatyard:

"Had so much caulking and painting to do last summer, didn't get the boat in the water once. Not going to happen this summer. Already made plans with five other boats to meet down the Bay in Jessup Moorings. Wife and I are going to take a long weekend. Take most of Friday to motor down. All day Saturday we'll fish, eat, get polluted. Come back home late Sunday night. It'll make the summer worth it!"

Sunday, 8 A.M.

I speak of silence
in our coastal village,
the absence of
hoarse mamas, gurgling papas,
late night gesticulations
troubadors in the sand pit
even trees wiggling—
all gone.
Now one gull cuts the sky
one sail on the Bay
clouds underscored with gray.
Then the light grows
stronger, golder.

House Hauntings

Since we have owned our house, we've had a variety of strange "infestations."

As a rule a squirrel would leap from a tree branch onto our roof with a startling thump around eight AM. We could put up with that enforced alarm clock. But one morning he sounded closer—scratching in the wall right above my desk. I phoned around to find a man who did not call himself an exterminator; he trapped an animal humanely and took it upstate to free it. He came and discovered the squirrel had crawled into the breezeway under the roof peak. Our "animal tamer" waited until the squirrel was out foraging before he set out his baited cage. Once the squirrel was caught, our expert hammered heavy gauge wire across any roof openings and took the varmint to his new environment.

We came downstairs one morning to find a heap of green-bottle flies dead on the floor as if a battle had occurred.

Another time a minutely straight trail of ants came from the casement, across the counter, and directly into one drawer. That's when we first got to know the ant exterminator whom we have been salarying everafter.

Arriving home from shopping we encountered a bat hanging from the backdoor light. I prodded him to discover he was quite alive; perhaps sleeping off a wild binge of mosquitoes. Fascinated, we worked around him with little inconvenience. He hung by that door for four days, even in daylight, before he was gone without explanation.

We even had a foot of water in the basement when heavy rains knocked out the electricity in town and our sump pump ceased to work. I carried out bucket after bucket from the sump hole; the cellar needed a thorough drying and repainting.

But the thing which haunted and frustrated us the most was the refrigerator which had turned eccentric. It was a rebuilt model but was tripping the circuits. Diagnosticians came and went with all kinds of ideas: from Freon capacity to just junking it and taking the loss. If we went away for a vacation, like a spoiled puppy the machine would act up and go off. We returned to ruined food too often.

I stood looking at it one day, imagining it a veteran with bandages and scars all over it—but still stubborn, arrogant, malignant. My wife and I glanced at each other: "Will they haul this one far away when we get the new one?" she whispered behind her hand so it couldn't read her lips.

On The Waterfront

Neon signs breed in
the inky riptide
which has decided
to come in to check
up on what's happening;
I walk between two
unlikely companions
—O'Neill and Conrad—
the first with wide red eyes
scoping out each swinging door,
the other searching for
a dry fireside, a pipe
and someone always there.

From a Daybook – II

I am feeling low, sitting in the living room. Then I see a spider's web hung from the rainspout, glowing. Trees dip in the wind and birds blow by like leaves. Sailboats slide past on the Bay. Sunlight slides across the floor. Why shouldn't I be?

Our house sits on the edge of town on a slope viewing the Bay. For years rain run-off has rutted several pieces of our land. Recently we hired Steve Lathbury to landscape. First he built a kind of dry river bed over the ruts, filled it with stones, then from it sank a drainage pipe out to the street culvert. He also tied our rainspouts into the pipe. All this diverting has worked. No longer a sump pump echoing its mournful rhythms throughout a rainy night.

Canoeing is an art on this Bay. We usually go in the morning. First we walk down to the shore, not to see if the tide is in or out, but to judge how smooth the surface is. For fun we sniff the air, scan the sky for clouds, check out bird formations flying over. However, choppy water can easily swamp a canoe; too choppy from nature or power boats. When we do launch we stay near shore, swinging wide around piers to avoid fishermen's lines. Little coves and inlets suit us best for tranquility and possible wildlife dramas.

Noticed that most people shy away from the town graveyard. But we find it serene and lovely in its own way. Stone angels with raised wings which the weather is slowly whittling down; mausoleum with glass doors where we can see drawers for family occupants (remember cartoon where passing couple see TV antenna on top?!). The dates on headstones capture complete town history. In spring someone has richly decorated some graves with flowers.

Scroungy dog came barking out of shadows at us one night as we walked. Some terrier in him but so mangy he is unpattable. Demeanor is independent and offsetting too. Now we see him everywhere as if he owned the town. Thought we found his owner who called "Max!" out of window, but saw him in another yard next day. Seems to stir up other dogs then skedaddles. Caught him eating dead squirrel by the Bay. Now we call him "squirrel-eater," shiver and try to avoid him.

Boat people from marina walk by in fair weather months. Some stop on the road and comment about our place. House is unique here on the Bay, a chalet meant for mountains, but we love its style and I guess some passers-by do too. We invite them in for tea if conversation proves interesting. Most boaters have a grand summer plan: pack in supplies and travel down the Bay as far as they can go in allotted vacation days.

The Hodges live on a high bluff where our two local rivers meet. Handy kind of guy, Roger Hodges has a greenhouse, sizable garden both flowers and vegetables, scads of birdfeeders. He loans out his log-splitter to anyone who can use it. Has a beautiful antique Franklin stove that works. Lately he's been experimenting with solar panels on his roof; saving a lot of money, he claims.

◇◇◇

Having walked around town so often in all seasons and all types of weather, we have fondly come to nickname some of the houses we see:

Fieldstone House, White Block House, Hollywood House, Miami House, Old Tree House, Cedar Shakes House, etc. But my favorite is what we call the Old Sea Captain's house; rectangular red brick, shuttered, almost flat roof with three dormers, stately chimneys at both ends. I imagine an old seaman in one of those third floor dormers training his telescope down the Bay toward the sea.

Poor Bill Moody, boy does some gardening for us. Both parents ran off when he was an infant. Grandparents raised him. His grandfather Justin is an honorable man, a policeman. Married 33 years. Then the grandmother decided to buy a motorcycle. Last week this gray-haired lady ran off with an old man she met in a bikers' club. Now they live "in sin" across the Bay in a trailer. Young Bill Moody carries on.

Birds on the Bay are a changing sight to be seen. In a row baby ducks sit on a water pipe from the marina, wise to and unscared by human ways. In the sky lines of geese and patches of gulls. A blue heron graces the end of a pier like a wrought-iron figurine. Sea birds bob like buoys far out, any season of the year.

The Shrink

His private trademark:
known in the city for
baldness, tallness, cigar,
all the week he traces
dark and clogged corridors.
Weekends inhales salt air
trots a desolate beach
listens to the parakeet speak
and pounds a muted piano.
A thing he has not cured,
his one tic: to be
first in his boat on
the Bay come spring.

Pastoral

Although they are trained to help others in need, ministers also being human are not exempt. I knew one from a wealthy upstanding family. His father before him had been a medical missionary to China. He trained many young Chinese who had potential. Fame came when he prepped an assistant to perform an appendectomy on him; it was totally successful and written up in journals round the world.

His father's achievements must have influenced our minister. As a little boy, he revered his father. The family had returned from China. Our minister's sisters were many years older. He often sat in the kitchen with the cook feeling like an only child; his mother's distancing from society didn't help much either.

He went off to a prestigious university; at the time biology was his number one love. Then Jesus called him as it does in mysterious unexplainable ways. He went to seminary, was appointed to a parish, and settled down to have a family.

Being a bright person he did well in the ministry: he earned an advanced degree in order to counsel individuals. His wife fully supported him. Summers they took their children to the Bay. He read, worked in the garden, and listened to opera on Sunday afternoons. He claimed that twenty-four hours there could completely renew him.

Then things began to go terribly awry: his older son went to college on the west coast and chose seldom to return home; his younger son got involved in drugs; and his only daughter had a nasty divorce. One day the stained glass in his church began to gesticulate; Jesus spoke to him in an unintelligible tongue. Our minister went to pieces.

His wife and he retired early to the Bay. He tried to read but could not concentrate. The garden no longer appealed to him. The last year of his life he spent in silence. He died of an unexpected heart attack while slouched in a hammock as a sailboat regatta took place just beyond his deck.

Mud-Flats

Moon's position has pulled tides
far out into the Bay.
Resembling a tar pit
mud-flats sparkling
in afternoon sun
densely fringed by seabirds.
Crow-talking beach grove
surrounded by mums
in a color spectrum.
Tonight under a half-moon
might we imagine
in the flats lies a hulk of boat,
maybe part of a torso.

Bay Festival

On a special day of the year between summer and fall, our little town came to life. The day began with a parade; a fife and drum corps, followed by Revolutionary soldiers who led George Washington on his prancing horse, bowing and doffing his tri-corn hat. Then high school bands, fire engines and rescue vehicles, waving local beauty queens on floats, a few waving local politicians in convertibles.

A mizzle hung in the air; that does not deter people who live close to the water. Food was prominent: Greek gyros, Mexican tacos, Italian hoagies, Polish kielbasa, Middle Eastern kabobs; soft pretzels, cheese steaks, angus burgers, funnel cake, corn-on-the-cob, cotton candy, water ice, homemade ice cream, pulled pork, and of course, crabs.

For children there were a carousel, Ferris wheel, tilt-a-whirl, magic show and pony rides; carriages for wannabe lovers, helicopter rides, parasailing, cruise on the "Mary Stewart." Three tents housed medieval smithing plus jousts and Morris dancers.

Booths stressed crafts connected with the sea: wooden duck decoys, canoe- making, water safety, local history and antique maps , and a boat raffle. Fortune- teller, photographs, silk flowers, paintings, macramé, jewelry, face-painting. A long row of classic autos. High on a platform country singers were amplified all over town.

Two cycle thugs duked it out till a cop arrived. Some teenagers stole packs of antique baseball cards successfully. Couple of babies threw up then went to sleep. When an old lady had a heart attack, the paramedics were already there and got cheered.

As night descended, out of the gloom the brightly lighted Ferris wheel continued to soar skyward, flags fluttering with excitement. The explosive conclusion to the weekend was fireworks over the Bay.

Shades of Gray

Pampas grass rubs heads
to make brushy music,
today a sad waltz
in diminished minors;
three shades of gray across
the Bay—sky, hills, water;
we're in for a nasty,
already air spits sleet
like a ruffian's challenge;
to last things out I need
a fix, what will it be—
jigsaw or crossword?
I want a single malt, neat!

To the Lighthouse

With another couple we were hiking down the peninsula to the local lighthouse, which was celebrating its 150th anniversary. The west side of this spit of land sharply fell off eighty feet into the Bay; the opposite side formed a gradual beach front. Near the entrance to the state park stood some private homes which backed up to the cliffs. We noticed one house with a free standing garage shaped like a delicate miniature Greek temple. We stopped to enjoy it and catch our breath.

The garage door opened and a man stepped out. He had an Abe Lincoln look— long arms and craggy benign face. "Looks like marble from a distance," he said, "but it's all wood." He beckoned us up the driveway. Ludicrously a sizable canopy bed was standing inside the garage. "I thought a woodworker's shop should look special," he laughed. He pointed to the bed. "This is a wedding gift for my son and his bride-to-be. All walnut. The touchiest part to do was those danged arched slats that support the canopy. Kept snapping on me till I learned a couple tricks about steaming wood."

He went on to tell us he had taken early retirement. We weren't surprised since in this exclusive area only the wealthy could afford these houses. But this man put on no airs. Another one of his joys was being one of several "reporters" who relay weather statistics twice a day to a TV station in the city. He measured the temperature, barometer, wind velocity and direction. The information was fed into computers and averaged for the nightly news show.

On top of that he and his son ("Young fella doesn't know a hammer from a hacksaw") babysat houses in the area. "Lots of wasted money around here," he said. "One house we check on has a flight of stairs—back stairs, mind you—each wide step was a different type of imported wood. Added up to $30,000! What a waste."

We shook heads and left with a wave. We fought our way through a jungle of tall old trees and vines which hung over the narrow path. We wore swarms of no-seeums around our faces.

Finally we came into the sunlight at the foot of the peninsula. The surf broke against the cliffs on three sides, and the breeze was strong, constant and fresh. The renovated lighthouse stood tall in its new coat of white paint, a landmark of time encapsulated. Some traditions were merely that; others were still active, ongoing into the future. The lighthouse had a broad view down the Bay. After that, there was nothing more to see.

On the way back we met a small wiry man with flushed face sitting on a boulder. We discovered that he lived where our families came from north of here a hundred miles. For a hobby he, too, coincidentally was a woodworker. "I had hung a hand-built door some years ago. As I was coming down the step-ladder, I caught my foot, fell, banged my head. From that day I couldn't taste or smell. Oh, sometimes I thought I could sniff a steak on the breeze. I was just fooling myself. Easy to stay thin now. Nothing tastes, all the glamour is gone, all I do is peck."

Tidewrack

I know I must get outside
not fear to breathe deep, yet
I know where books are hidden
like whiskey bottles stashed
or loaded pistols
just to kill the time;
in the sun's morning bath
blades of grass are tingling,
dead leaves mingling
a zombie slumber party,
tidewrack brings in the news
sways in the past, saves
tomorrow for the future.

The Good Life

The estate was named Solidad and sat on top of a hill. However, it was far from being anti-social. Night and day cars snaked up and down the long driveway. In summer girls in bikinis in and out of the pool; men in shorts with tennis racquets or in business suits. In the game room was heard the clack of pool balls, the tock of ping pong, while half-dressed people danced to the vintage juke box. Like a birthday cake the yacht was moored in the harbor until the season for dry dock.

The circular living room boasted a domed glass ceiling and pink marble floor. A huge stone fireplace reared up and a fountain gushed, which made conversation difficult. The house was of Asian design, so it was unique to observe the contrasting French rococo furniture.

Many years before, three brothers started a drugstore. Becoming successful, they opened others and also bought several small radio stations in the region. Their final coup was to purchase majority shares in some Japanese shoe factories. Bucky and Barry, the blessed sons of one of the enterprising brothers, were sent to boarding school then to the state college. At eighteen Dad gave each of them Jaguar roadsters, one black one white. Bucky loved the lever you could pull to avoid the muffler and get a straight through roar. Barry, the older brother, went to try his luck at acting in Hollywood; a substantial allowance supported him. He seldom came home again. Bucky became a manager in one of his father's firms.

Bucky was beloved by females. He enjoyed being the eternal prankster. At a party he would wander around with fly unzipped and shirttail sticking out until a girl giggled and hugged him to her breast. As he grew older, Bucky dated one tall slender blonder after another.

The two boys' mother flitted like a ghost through the mansion usually wearing a tatty housecoat, faded red hair in curlers. She avoided guests, her English disguised by a nondescript European accent. You would have to stare deeply to ascertain what beauty the boys' father found in her. However, it was rumored that he had a long line of "hostesses" in various countries he frequented on business.

Ethel, the head of housekeeping, lounged in the kitchen where all the appliances looked as if made from chrome. "If you had told me I'd work here for eighteen years, I'd never have believed it," she said. "But the Mister and Missus have been very good to me. Can't say the pay is bad either. The two boys I've treated as my own."

Racing a Lamborghini on a back road one night, Bucky hit a stone wall. The auto exploded and all the authorities found were his legs. Church services were local. It was gratifying to see that a large group of people came to pay their respects.

Unseen Forces

The Bay was running
strong in silver waves
as a force swooped over
esker, dumlin, moraine
through heather and bayberry
juniper and chokeberry;
in all its vulnerability
the white-washed house stood
alone on the dunes
devoid of foliage,
giving the feeling that
what happened inside
would be etched on outer walls.

The Voice

He's been dead such a short time. Even so, I can't recall his voice. His diction, yes, his use of special phrases, but not his actual voice. I could say soprano or gravelly, but that wouldn't do at all. It's like three women commentators I hear on radio. One sounds like a cute but wise little girl. Another sounds like a tall and slender proper British woman. The third is earthy, full of life, a healthy jogger who was captain of the cheerleading team. I don't want to see them; I am sure I will be dreadfully wrong. I couldn't watch Sesame Street anymore with my kids because the voices of Kermit, Miss Piggy, and the gang had changed. Can one be so sensitive as to fall in love with a voice, a sound? I don't think it can be done with a taste, an aroma, a touch. Perhaps in power sound does equal sight. How often we are disappointed when we hear a recording of our own voice. I would rather listen to the ocean speak in all its moods. Even the seagull has a number of voices he can speak in.

I have to make this aside here, since you, the reader, have been patient enough to read this far. Fiction isn't real as we know it. Notice how events happen smoothly in stories. What happened before the story began; what will happen after it's over, because life doesn't stop. The boy gets off the train to meet his girl. However, in real life he had to wait for that train, then the train ride was long and tedious. What did he do moment to moment in that time span? It's boring so forget it. Also, listen to real talk—the pauses, misstatements, repeats, floundering for words, etc. The writer cleans it all up for the purpose of smoothness, to sell the story.

Thanksgiving Day

Down gray throat of inlet
there is only water,
not one launch to dare the Bay.
Water so still night lights
stretch nearly across,
as sound would travel miles
over frozen flatlands.
Action found in houses
wrapped in aromas,
outside of windows sleet,
inside children's breath.
All day pops of goose guns
to bring home the feast.

Getting Ready

There are different ways to get ready. Getting ready for summer, you open windows, hammer down recalcitrant nails, take out the umbrella, oil the wooden table, sling the hammock. In summer there is an exploding and reaching out; you want to be naked. However, autumn is a drawing in for security, making a nest.

Sometime in early autumn something clicks in me. I feel I'm getting ready for a happening.

I prune the indoor plants, repotting where needed, tossing away when hopeless.

I polish my shoes and set them in a row on the hardwood floor to gleam in the sunlight.

I clean my briar pipes much as a homemaker would polish silver.

I make sure the car is tuned up.

I sweep the garage.

I hold summer pants up to the light to check for any thinness.

I jot down any interesting books, people, ideas I've recently encountered and put them in a file box.

I walk round and round the house inside and out, as if caught in a cycle. I'm searching for fix-up projects.

When I take the canoe out on the Bay, I keep thinking it might be the last. Perhaps the swells will be too high—and not from power boats; the wind will cut too cold and deep; or simply a coating of ice on the Bay will prevent me from launching.

This must all sound a bit compulsive. I guess it is. It's just my way of marking and celebrating the change of seasons.

Mistaken Identity

Cold has blown away
summer activities,
beach desolate except
against a boarded cabin
flags and rags on a line
come to a kind of life
in occasional breeze;
half-viewed through porch railing
the scene becomes a small
group of people partying,
adjusting one leg over
another, tossing long hair
waving arm to make a point.

Gossip

I had been away for a week: just enough time to let a local story grow and gel. One of the best places to hear a nice piece of gossip is in the post office. After all, the post office is where the news arrives and is sent. Also, this post office still retains an historical feeling with its walnut paneling, brass fixtures, even quaint shutters on windows. Soon enough gossip becomes historic.

Seems as if one afternoon in Breeze (Point Breeze, a town on the other side of the Bay where cliffs are steep) a trailer truck was coming down the incline of the main street. The street runs into the town square, and if you'd keep walking, you'd be on the dock.

A normal afternoon kids are playing in the square, lovers holding hands, old people sitting in whatever shade they could find.

At the crest of that grade, the driver suddenly realized his brakes were failing. As he careened down the hill he began to lean on the air horn. The square cleared fast, and that semi must have hit the square at over one hundred miles per hour. People testified they saw only a blur, he was wailing so fast.

The truck sent the statue of Captain Ramsey sailing like a shot. It landed in someone's garden, jammed head first, his rusty copper legs quivering.

Due to the driver's straight maneuvering, down the pier he went, took a huge leap and plunged into the Bay as smooth as a pro's swan dive. The self-reliant driver—being small as well as wily—got out a window and emerged unharmed.

A couple days later, cranes first hauled up the cab then the truck, filled with twenty thousand pounds of vegetables.

You could trace the neat course of the truck by its tire tread, not marring even a bush, not to say the Captain—but not one person hurt. A definite tale to savor and embroider for its suspense; without tragic shadings.

Lunar History

I cannot face the fury of
the sun—moon I talk to.
Your paleness well describes
the dying of numerous
lovers' passionate hopes.
Like the ravaged landscape
many wars have you watched.
You can alter our tides
yet weaken with the month
obscured by mists of time.
But you always return
—pity us if you don't—
compassionate as ever.

Still Life

What makes me love this painting of a snow-covered town? It's not by a grand artist. Just someone with a very good pictorial eye. And a heart that includes very poignant human things in his painting. In proper artistic terms this painting is a landscape, but the life—caught in a microcosm—is the most important element to deem it "a still life."

Lights glowing brightly from windows on the main street of this small town contrast sharply with the threatening grayness of another possible winter storm coming.

Among the rows of stores are two cottages which belong in the country. Is this typical? However, their ground levels offer display windows, so they fit in. Chimneys are puffing all along the street like men with pipes around a pot-bellied stove in a club.

Maybe another touch of exaggeration might be the outdoor warmth. Although plenty of new fallen snow (no gray slush to suggest old snow) on roofs, awnings, streets, sidewalks, and what must be grassy open areas, people are standing in small groups passing the time of day. One girl is even reclining on a low stone wall. Yet persons in this climate must be used to snow.

Then the painter is perceptive enough to dab in tiny realistic touches: a wandering trail over a snowy lawn whether made by human or animal; and a surface of the sidewalk turned to ice which shines in the lamplight like a jagged mirror; also one dog standing erect staring at something, as dogs are wont to do.

Call this painting too typically realistic, or too far-fetched for real. I'm sure down a side street within a block or two lies the Bay. I can almost sniff the salt air. What would this painter's interpretation of that be?

Dawn to Dusk

Lawns and fields will be laid waste
till spring not to be visited,
there like a rough chessboard
sleet and snow, hail and gale
will contend, checking
innocent things in their grip;
yet these autumn days are wrapped
in bookends of gold
timid dawn, sighing dusk,
at twilight our Bay
pulls on a silver coverlet,
nothing else in sight
except the hopes of men.

Cold

An old man speaks:

Cold! You want to know how cold it used to get? The Bay could be vicious in foul or cold weather. That's why all the dockages and marinas are upriver. The streams and inlets froze solid.

Some places of the world have skiing, high speed skating, ice carving. Here you could walk across the ice to the town on the far shore. Wind cut you in half. Snow dust was as thick as fog. On a clear day sun glare could blind you. Midway across you felt as if you were at sea. Felt it was breaking up under foot, you were on an ice flow; only imagination. You half expected to meet Jack London out there or the Frankenstein monster or Little Eva.

Jeeps dragged fishing shacks onto the ice. You cut your hole, set the shack over it, and put in a portable stove. Each roof wore a top hat. Didn't forget to bring a six- pack or flask. Could fit three or four fellas in there pretty snug.

Had jeep races on the ice. Even sled dog races; teams came from miles around. Funny thing about ice or snow: you could be having a conversation in normal voice and they could hear you crystal clear a mile away down the Bay.

On shore the trees turned to glass; some splintered. Icicles hung from house eaves like a long line of fish curing. A snowman all winter in the yard next door gets to you; like an obnoxious neighbor. Snow didn't melt till way into spring. Each storm the snow plows just tamped it down. When the ice began to break up, the sounds were supernatural.

I must interrupt again to quote Jonathan Raban's definition: "It accommodates the private diary, the essay, the short story, the prose poem, the rough note and polished table talk with indiscriminate hospitality. It freely mixes narrative and discursive writing. Much of the factual material, in the way of bills, menus, ticket- stubs, names and addresses, dates, and destinations, is there to authenticate what is really fiction; while its wildest fictions have the status of possible facts. Because of this general confusion, it has always been a favorite haunt of writers, just as critics, with some justification, have usually regarded it as a resort of easy virtue."

Raban is defining travel writing. However, what you are reading is not travel; the Bay stays in one place, although beneath the surface, as in one's mind, things are always in motion.

Crystal Sky

Man-made structures motionless
humans strangely absent
plants in a terrarium
the air crystalline;
a seagull seems whiter
purer than proverbial dove
in its aloneness,
the Bay nearly ready
to be coated by a mirror;
sky an onyx dome
under which the elite
in glittering finery
used to minuet.

The Gay Year

Ed Steinbacher was as close to the image of a Prussian as you could get. He seldom spoke, walked stiffly erect and always held a scowl on his face. What Maggie, who was the sweetest, most humble woman in the world, saw in him none of us could figure out. Perhaps she didn't know either; and that might have been the answer to it.

Ed, however, was a carpenter's carpenter, a woodworker in art. He lived in the oldest house in town. Every piece of that house, if it was wood and needed replacement, he had handmade in his shop, a shed in the corner of their property.

He did allow a family reunion on the place every year. Dozens of cousins played with his kids, games were devised, a lot of picnic food and beer for the adults. But the kids skirted around Ed in silence. Over the years he had made wooden Christmas presents for the clan until they became repetitive.

A couple nights a week Ed would stop by a local taproom for a beer, stand in the corner, then in a few moments be gone. After the children had grown up and left, Ed started wandering down to the docks to see the fishing boats going out or coming in. Maggie noticed the change. Was it for the good or bad.

She hadn't been in his shop for years, so she went when he was away. The size of the shop seemed to have dwindled; things were still neat but fewer. She wondered what the coil of thick black hose, maybe six feet long, was for in the corner. On her way out she was shocked to see that the hose was now on the other side of the room and extended. She never went there again.

One night around Christmas Ed came home with a young man. By his looks he was a sailor; he had a duffle bag over a shoulder. Ed told Maggie to get all her clothes out of the bedroom. She stared at the sailor who only returned her look with a half- smile. The two men climbed the stairs and slammed the bedroom door.

What could Maggie do? Where could she go? She didn't understand anything, so she slept that night on the sofa. She felt embarrassed and ashamed. Her children seldom called but what could she say. As the weeks passed the meals were now for three, but the silence was no different. At night from her sofa in the living room, the most she heard now and then from behind that closed door was the sailor's muffled chuckle. The two men would be in the shop for most of the day. Maggie's loneliness and discomfort were almost unbearable, but she took care of the house since she knew nothing else.

About a year later, when she had come back from shopping, the bedroom door was open and the duffle bag gone. She walked through the house. Ed was in the living room quietly smoking, an unusual place for him to do that. What's for dinner? he asked, which was another first.

Ice Bay

We go down to the beach
to see frozen plates
to guess where the tide lurks;
huge chunks of diamonds
veins within the freeze
and even trapdoors;
graffiti way out there
footsteps and dog prints
sled marks into the distance;
we keep moving so
our blood won't coagulate,
crows and gulls chuckling
at how balmy it feels.

Hurricane

When I was a child, I was in a hurricane on the Jersey shore. That was before they tried to humanize these monsters by giving them male or female names. There was little warning in those days; suddenly a gray roaring was on you. That was all you remembered, except for the praying. The sea ate up the beach and turned the walls of our rented house into sagging bilious green rubber. People on the floor below us stayed long enough to see their furniture floating and mice skittering. We barely escaped inland to relatives with our lives.

The Bay is solid protection from direct ocean assaults; in two hundred and fifty years our town has never had a lethal storm. And yet Hurricane Isabelle tried its worst. Some boat people thought they were safer having their vessels under a marina's tin roof. But when the tidal surge hit, it smashed the boats up against the ceiling. And when the wave withdrew, they collapsed on momentary dry Bay bed. Some boats found themselves on lawns in odd positions.

Water Street reclaimed its name because people were rowing and canoeing on it. The deed to our house stated that the flood plain extended to only the tip of our property; it was absolutely accurate. Other people were scurrying around taking photos to back up their future insurance claims. The weird thing about a storm like this is it is so intense while it is happening; then suddenly it's gone and the next day is sunny and strangely silent.

I saw people wandering around whom I had never seen before in town; as if only a cataclysm like this could get them out of a back room and away from the bottle or laptop. Good moments did happen: without electricity townsfolk shared food with each other. A line of riprap circled the town to show how far the Bay had invaded. But no homes were destroyed. The lowest point of land was then an empty lot. Now two McMansions sit there. As if we learned from the ants, nothing stops man from building.

What's Left

What's left in winter
now snow has been rolled
away for a while,
afternoon gold on the grass,
strands of ivy green
and green pine clusters;
smell of summer sweat
in an old ball cap,
song on the radio
heard last in July heat,
the Bay looking more
like iceberg Alaska
but remember.

Loser

The body was found floating face down, the long hair spread out around the head like seaweed. It was between two boats moored in the marina among the bubblers in the icy water. The coroner was investigating the possibility of foul play

Chip grew up next to the Bay. His father was an on again off again fisherman the length of the Bay. His mother was pretty much a habitual drunk. As a matter of fact, his father did not want to come home to find her sober because she was stony, he used to say.

Chip grew up as much as any other kid in that time when opportunities were lean. When he was a pre-teen, he put on a lot of weight and developed a serious case of acne. He also accused his uncle—a former Marine and happy father of three children—of child molestation. Since the state gave little leeway to what was considered a loathsome crime, his favorite uncle served a lengthy sentence.

As a young man Chip drifted from job to job. He worked longest as sous-chef in a crab restaurant. He was fired for showing up late and disheveled. But he liked the feel of a good suit. He longed to be a pit boss in Vegas. He even saved up enough money to go west to get training as a dealer. However, he couldn't seem to memorize the card sequences and washed out.

Back on the Bay he thought his experience in the real world would finally bring him luck. On a shoe string he rented a small store which he stocked with imported coffee, tea, chocolate. He reasoned that the flush tourists would miss what they couldn't get back in the big city. Chip hadn't considered the long winter with no tourists. He just about stayed alive by mostly selling lottery tickets to locals.

By this time he couldn't afford his own apartment. He owed a lot of people money. He took up with an older boat woman who liked younger men. Chip could manipulate her fairly well with the whiskey she had him buy.

That's where our story comes full circle, or rather to an abrupt halt. Although we have a quite extensive list of suspects, the coroner and

D.A. decided against foul play. While drunk or stoned or both, Chip had struck his head against some part of the moored boat, fallen into the water and drowned. With some persuasion the woman who owned the boat covered burial expenses.

Desert Island

This is the closest to
my sense of heaven,
sky the shade of pure milk.
With an orchestra of surf
in rips and eddies and swirls
birds warble angelically.
Sea cave in shape of
cathedral sometimes submerged
other times rising in the sun
as a proclamation.
Naked and cleansed by air
untainted for thousands of miles,
I float on this island cloud.

Pipes

What better companion to walk on the dock or pounded winter beach, to sit on a deck with than a pipe. One thing about pipe-smoking—they know you've been there. The aroma—be it sweet like cherry or walnut—or distinctive like the slightly charred quality of latakia—hangs reminiscently on the air. Pipe smoke is not acrid like cigar or innocuous like cigarette which is no more distinct that a ghost trying to communicate.

Looking at my row of pipes brings wafting back warm memories. I had sent away one dollar to a New York company for a saddle billiard. As it broke in, the once smooth surface revealed little holes filled with putty. But no matter, for it has burned clear and true (taking into mind occasional cleanings) for many years.

A pipe I had silver-banded in Boston which—I felt and still do—made it much more handsome than its original homeliness. Some years afterward, I bought a lovat when I had traveled farther afield to England for the first time. Then I was presented for my birthday a prestigious Dunhill; but I find it no better than any of my other pipes.

Some pipes remain unique; others a pain—like an eccentric personality you both admire and dislike simultaneously. I find my pipe with the military bit to be admirable. It is said that if you drop it, the stem will invariably pop free to prevent breaking. I haven't tried that rather demonstrative test—I just like the way it looks. A beloved uncle gave me a full-bent he had smoked in college; that in itself made a fifty year old heirloom.

The meerschaum a friend brought back from Africa has a veneer. True white meerschaum can be easily discolored by fingers; however, I wasn't about to wear gloves. But this yellow-coated one hasn't gained any character for it refuses to darken. I bought a bulldog shape that is meerschaum-lined; that's the extent I wish to indulge myself in meerschaum.

I tried to sand down a three-quarter bent, plum colored pipe to its natural wood, so I could observe the darkening process. Ever since, I have regretted having destroyed that singular purple hue.

Time does change all things. I have never ruined a pipe—breaking no more than an easily replaceable stem. I have heard horrible tales of pipe-smokers reaming holes through their bowls with cleaning instruments or mauling finishes by knocking out their pipes against rough walls.

I found that I grew dissatisfied with an apple shape—it began to look just too plump—so I gave it away. Mysteriously another pipe developed a crack on the lip of its bowl. I guess that heat will gradually lengthen the crack until the bowl breaks; it will be interesting to observe science at work. On the philosophical side of things, I have found that pipes force time to trot more slowly.

Beside the Dragon

Living at the shore feels like
lying beside a dragon
who roars and ripples
turns and curls over and
over, never settled.
In summer dragon's breath
crawls over the beach and
inland to sear the earth
its scales scorching skin.
Winter ashen skies
foretell a rising of
the dragon whose fury
inverts the world in ice.

Menage a Trois

My wife and I were taking a nighttime stroll. Suddenly a skinny old man came lurching out of a house. Tufts of hair stood up on his head like antennas as he waved his arms wildly.

"Are you Randy?" he squawked.

"No, I'm not."

"Well, I've been looking for him!"

I moved between him and my wife. "I can't help you."

"The bastard owes me money."

We started to continue down the street when I got a better glimpse at him in the moonlight. He was waving a revolver.

Just then a white-haired woman emerged from the same door.

"Now, Gus, that's not Randy. Come back in the house."

"Well, that bastard owes me money."

"Leave those people alone."

"I've got something for that goddamn..." She herded him off.

That was our first meeting with Gus; but his story was a long one in the town.

Gus had owned a marina that had gone to pot. Drinking became his major employer. In her way his wife Molly was more successful. Her cookbooks were selling well along the Bay. In a normal sad story that would pretty much be the end of it. However, another woman had moved in with them.

Ellen had been an old friend of Molly's, and now she was living with them. Tall and distant she wobbled as she walked. Talk had it that the two women slept in the same bed. Gus had moved down the hall because of his loud snoring.

But his boasting in local bars led the regulars to believe he was servicing both of them; three old people in a menage a trois. Who really knew? One night they found Gus in his lone bed, having choked to death. No autopsy was performed.

The two women still inhabit that grand old brick house, getting shabbier every year. They seldom come outside. They do their shopping by car, just like an old married couple, in a town across the Bay.

Night of Old Snow

Tonight haloes surround
every streetlamp.
On the Bay a barge
is strung with colored lights.
Leftover snow sends up
its last gasps in mist.
In the old part of town
a red store front door hangs
half-off its hinges.
No living thing wants
to leave its bit of warmth,
as dampness lumbers
down the lane.

Logo

A logo is defined as a symbol. It seems that from his very beginnings, Man has thought in terms of logos. Take the Lescaux cave paintings of 40,000 years ago. The unknown artist was not trying to paint a literal representation of an animal on the cave wall. He was giving his own abstract impression of that deer, bear, wooly mammoth.

The first languages were cuneiform and hieroglyphics. You can see all kinds of figures in Egyptian and Mayan inscription, from men to animals to daily working tools to surreal gods.

During the Middle Ages logos reached a high point. Knights wanted to celebrate their family histories; a crest, a coat-of-arms which would last an eternity. Colors were carefully selected: green=nature, purple=kingship, gold=wealth, blue=wisdom. Shields were painted in halves, thirds, quarters; each section held a logo. A tree could represent the knight's forest, an outline of his castle, a cross his religion, and so it went.

Similarly in Asian gardens an upright stone was a chain of mountains, a tiny pond was the ocean, neatly raked pebbles the entire earth, and a short winding path one's years of life.

In your imagination stroll down an 18th century American street to find signs swinging in the breeze. A needle for the tailor, anvil for the blacksmith, mug for the local pub. And the barber pole, along with the pawnshop's three balls, have lasted into the present day.

In the 1950s to jump on the Ivy League bandwagon, you wore a tiny belt on the back of your pants but ran the risk of scratching your mother's dining room chair if you leaped to get the hall phone . But with your emblems you were in style.

Today we walk around covered with logos: our caps, tee shirts, sandals, sunglasses, blankets, cups, etc.—mostly to sell that product. And specifically what logos symbolize our Bay? Light house, sailboat, pier, blue heron or egret, myriad sea creatures ranging from crab to sailfish.

Ideal Bay

I don't want my Bay
to be squeezed by concrete,
nor populated by
a forest of vessels;
I want to smell shrubbery,
plants, and healthy mudflats,
perhaps a hint of brine
beckoning down the Bay;
I want to find ancient cairns,
eat and sleep in its
upperrighthand corner,
then swim the length of
twilight's golden rectangle.

Not a Stripper

Daisy was a feather dancer. No, not fans, not bubbles. She would get furious if you suggested she was a stripper. She wore a tutu. She had taken ballet lessons and modern dance, such as it was back then. She was an "artiste." Her mother always told her, End up standing up.

Daisy had been on the road for some time. She earned a good living but worked hard for it, one act in a sizable troupe. It was Omaha where she was introduced to Jake Payton. He was impressive at the very first meeting. You could tell he was a well-to-do businessman: mustache, tailored suit, even a carnation in his button hole. However, Daisy was taken by the gorgeous camel's hair topcoat

He was also taken by her. She encountered him in a couple cities on her itinerary and was awestruck by his dedication. He told her he had owned a number of restaurants then sold them all for great profit. He asked for her hand on a sunny terrace in a Nevada hotel.

Together they bought the Bellwood Club right on Graysheep Bay. It had a proud heritage where people like Teddy Roosevelt and Howard Taft visited in winter to hunt duck. Jake was going to make it a year-round resort. He improved the marina, put in the first swimming pool in the area, a nine-hole golf course, gave his workers healthy raises. He let Daisy introduce a special dish—Oysters Rockefeller—a recipe her mother had taught her was sure-fire.

Over the next years the place indeed did grow. Daisy became an adroit social hostess. An oil painting of her in full feather hung in one of the ornate dining rooms. If you looked at the portrait years later, Daisy changed little. She kept her figure and the perfect texture of that Irish skin.

She also learned to give Jake room for he was a fair but hard line manager. He was fond of her, but she knew he did not want her dabbling in the business. He started to complain about profits even when the restaurant was full. Once she happened to enter his office, saw his desk drawer heaped with cash, but fled at his curses.

Then Jake Payton died of a sudden heart attack. Daisy soon

discovered that they had debts. She tried her best to run the place. Her oldest clients rallied round. But the building grew shabby. Her little dogs ran rampant in the kitchen. Her sister came to assist her but with her weight and eye problems was little help. Then the sister also died.

Over and over Daisy told her few customers the story of the Commander: "One day I was coming down the main stairs of the Bellwood. It was winter so all the windows were closed, but the drapes over our large picture window were tossing about. I stopped right there on the stairway and in no uncertain terms said, Commander, You've been dead for two hundred years. There's no need to make a fuss now!"

Archaeological

In spring is the time
for archaeology
along country roads.
Among obvious artifacts
a bumper part signals
icy incident.
Tiny delicate bones
reveal a rodent
not finding his burrow.
Shrink-wrapped haystacks in
fields and mummified
vessels in the boatyard
wait for rebirth.

Ornis

He is the grand old man, as free Germany referred to its president, Conrad Adenauer, as "der alte." And the French to DeGaulle, or even America to Lincoln: tall, rangy, silent—unless he had something pertinent to say. That is the blue heron, who has the shape of a black lightning bolt. He stands on one leg motionless, contemplating the universe. He utters little. Each step is premeditated and slow as he moves toward his prey. When humans get too close, he flaps to another jetty, seemingly unperturbed. He never seems in a hurry, flustered, or even lonely.

Crows are the boys on the corner, just out of the pool hall. Dressed in black caps, black turtlenecks, tight black pants, with yellow sneaks. They hang around in trees, cackling jokes, giving the raspberry, chuckling bawdily. Telling tales from tree to tree then drifting off till only one remains.

Gulls always look so clean , their grays and whites immaculate, gleaming in the sunlight. Yet they scavenge and fight for what they can get. They move in groups like a snow shower. In winter they huddle on a marina tin roof for warmth. If you listen to them long enough, you realize how many words, voices they have: from the cry of a baby to the mournful begging call in the wake of a ship.

Lots of other types live in our town. Flocks of grackles clicking and shiny like mother-of-pearl on the lawn. Geese grazing with their fierce sentries posted. Plovers , love chokers around their necks, standing on such skinny stilts you wonder why they don't snap. The osprey who in its gigantic nest utters the most childlike tweet. The daffiest of them all, the wise guy mockingbird who eyes you, tries out some of his many words, calculates, then flies away on striped wings just as you get interested.

One of my fondest encounters with birds was this side of unbe-lievable. Sitting on my porch one day, I spotted a tiny couple—male and female mallards—waddling up the quiet lane. They deliberately turned into my driveway and came halfway up, eyeing me. After a calculated waiting period when I had nothing to donate, they turned around, continued up the street, and into the next driveway.

These are the "residents" who live around here. And have been here for longer than we by thousands of years. We are the squatters. We don't speak their language but can at least try to get to know their ways.

On the Bridge

Just like a cold day
air in this room feels harsh,
fabrics faded like
winter vegetation;
then I remember
we came from ocean
so veins of the Bay
sustain and remind us;
on the bridge people read
the air, hovering in space
between immensities,
one way watching the past,
other the future.

From a Daybook – III

Sun reveals all in this coastal village. It is merciless and tactlessly honest. It shows homely people as they are, or wrinkles. It spotlights cracks in the ground, on walls, and in hearts. This is not a travel piece. No tourists come here. The sailors work hard and sincerely. This is a homely little port tucked away in a fold of the huge Bay. Only the odor of cooking garlic in the afternoon. A few crooked streets. But readers don't want too much setting, too many things described. They want a story, a story never heard before. Or better yet, they want to learn about people, real people—and thus, themselves.

If one were to describe flowers, color is only part of their attraction. Imagine the shape of hollyhocks in the garden or asparagus ferns. It would make a reader think twice to see bamboo through the window, if not the Far East. Smells crawl over the windowsill, beckoning to you at dusk. But flowers are a pure abstraction. A writer runs a real risk to deal with them at all.

A case could be made that birds are the most animated things in nature. Think of the deep luminescence of a bluebird. The repertoire of a mockingbird is close to the ensemble of an eighteenth century orchestra. Yet color and song are only parts of a bird's worth. Swallows soar like planes. A finch performs a series of dips. Then suddenly it is night and cicadas begin to sing in their unique way.

On a clear day at dusk, there is a moment when sun throws a light on the Bay where it shows the bones, the very sinews, then settles into darkness like a duck settling into his own feathers for sleep.

We have slipped away from people and their stories; what the reader wants most to relate to. Let us enter a large old city. The city is totally man-made. A library stands in the midst of a thousand thousand choices. It is a castle of brick and tiled roof with caryatids gracing the cornices. In addition the plate glass windows prove its modernity. A library is a perfect place for here this writing becomes a book within books.

A painting by Maurice Vlaminck hangs on the wall. Would it make any difference to know he was born in Reuil-la-Gadeliere? that he was a cyclist? lived to be 82 years old? or his friend was Derain? Vlaminck's painting shows a small house on the edge of an unnamed village caught in a storm. It is Impressionism, but Vlaminck went on into Cubism and ended in Abstract Expressionism. He was known as a "wild beast" to other men.

Brahms' Third Symphony is a world. The first movement is a world in itself. That movement offers a majestic opening with strong recurring themes from violins and woodwinds. One hears quick moody sections then even faster passages. Textures are dense. In the second movement the woodwinds play a slow almost bucolic melody. Then overwhelming sadness by the violins echoed by the brass in the third section. The final movement returns to majesty, tempo and shading strongly defined. A final crescendo but resolved in softness.

But where are we? Is the reader satisfied? Have we not left the world of things and contemplated Man's creations. How close can we get to reality than in a play, a fabrication of real life. Here in this living box we see day and night, feel summer and winter. Listen to Man's wisdom: "I never travel without my diary. One should always have something sensational to read in the train." It's the importance of being as earnest as we can.

Yet, a vital piece is missing. The most vital. The reader wants the writer to reveal himself in some way. The ultimate intimacy: to hear the writer's point-of-view. "I observe. I live." So to close I will tell you about an old man I knew sitting on a farmhouse porch clinging to the side of a mountain. The old man leaned back in his creaking chair, having finished a glass of iced tea but still holding it in both hands probably for the coolness. It had been an unusually warm summer. Perhaps it brought things up out of memory that ordinarily would have lain dormant till death.

"Know what's up the mountain?" he asked with a thumb pointed to clarify.

"Family graveyard," I said surely.

"What else?" His eyes became slits with a kind of merriment I'd barely seen in
them before.

I stumbled, "Er, the spring which feeds the house by gravity flow."

"Something else, young one."

"I don't know."

"Upper meadow," he said. "Used to be a powerful lot of love-making in that upper meadow."

Winter Misc.

Bayside backyard
intriguing mix of
sand, dead leaves, rocks, logs.
Temperature just above freezing
so it can rush back to touch
base if necessary.
Lincoln's birthday
heavy odor of flowers
hanging on cemetery air.
In a building by the pier
the crack of pool balls
and a whine on TV split
the frosted silence.

Break In

We had been away on vacation for a week. As soon as we entered, my wife sensed something was not right. I was slow on the up-take. "Someone has been in this house!" she whispered. Then we noticed a little statue in the bookcase was lying on its side. We scoured the house. Missing: a fine pair of binoculars, a flashlight, an old Spanish dagger I used as letter-opener. Yet every window and door was locked.

When the state troopers arrived, they were surprised. "You mean nothing else is missing?" They too searched the house and even outside. "You know what real thieves do? Maybe you don't want to know, but you should for your own education. You were lucky." My wife sat on the couch shivering.

"They want you to know they were here. That's part of the power trip. They stop up your toilets and let them overflow. They have fun starting a fire in the middle of your floor. If it gets out of control, so what. They scrawl lewd messages on the walls. Then they steal what they can hock." The police concluded that these were amateurs who wanted easy access and probably wouldn't try again.

That didn't make it any easier. The following nights I had nightmares of shadowy figures looming over our bed. We wondered over and over how they got in without broken locks. I guess we couldn't be absolutely sure every window and door had been secure. We had the locks changed.

Then one day my wife remembered that we had given an extra key to our neighbors for an emergency when we were away. We checked with them. They hardly recalled the transaction. They too had been broken into some months back but could find nothing stolen. However, they couldn't locate our key. The thieves must have read the tag and tried for better pickings nextdoor.

The police returned no stolen property. The feelings of vulnera-bility and helplessness slowly subsided. However, at the end of the month we received a phone bill for over $100.00 to Fiji; seems the robbers had also made some pornographic calls. We are still adjusting.

Midwinter on the Bay

Where ice lay last week
lights on the far shore
form bridges across water;
a shadow on the wall,
I listen for any sounds
left over from summer;
only a mournful gull
some cynical crows
wind's meow through a pipe;
sunsets private but
still a spectacle;
remaining heat in red stripes
on flag forgotten in the square.

Town Meeting

I enjoy attending the monthly town meeting. I take a large thermos of coffee, perhaps laced with a dram or two of John Jameson. I also take a pillow to combat the hard upright wooden chairs. I sit in the rear of the hall with my spine against the shadowed wall.

Beaulieu's voice is like a canary; Crowley rumbles like a bullfrog. I can't understand either of them. Davis is the chairman. He has been on and off the committee in different capacities for over twenty years. With a little campaigning you can usually win a seat; few people in town like the boredom or small power of the job. Davis has been known as a philanderer. He winks at all women no matter their race, religion, age or preferences. He winks before and after he talks to them, or when they talk to him on the committee.

Usually the group discusses issues like dredging the beach front, repairing the town's chain link fence, how often the sheriff patrols at night, whether water quality is up to par. The eternal proposal to buy or not buy a new snow plow has been postponed for years now and has become a national village myth.

The biggest item on the agenda has been brewing for a few months. The zoning committee claims that, yes, Mr. Walters attained a valid building permit, but his structure is nearly six feet in height over the town's limit. Walters is his own attorney; he's not bad for a local businessman who knows the right people. He claims out of "the bigness of his heart" that he built the extra room above his garage for his mother-in-law "who is failing." Could he help it that he went "overboard out of caring?" His wife "wanted the best" for her mother, and you all know how Marjorie is—"full out or nothing." And May (his m-i-l) needs the room, being "generous in size."

Sometimes it is hilarious and very entertaining. Sometimes, I must admit, I nod off. When I suddenly came to, I thought I was in an old movie house. The film was about a small town; Jimmy Stewart was debating with Lionel Barrymore; Zasu Pitts was screaming at Charlie Rutherford. Davis' gavel finally descended.

February Warm Up

A giant boy has left
jigsaw pieces of ice
strewn across the harbor,
mews of gulls fluttering the air
gabbling snow floes of ducks;
someone has brushed grayness
in a firm broad stroke
across the horizon,
dabbed smudges like ever-
green beyond the dim Bay;
we walk with bold intent,
hoods tossed back, salty dampness
in brows and lashes.

Time to Spring

Spring is about tears: the sudden squall of a child who wants something now. Or the mournful weeping of a bereaved mother; muted, almost not there at all unless you give full attention. Drops on the window pane or gushings of basins which give way to sun streaks in moments.

With my hurt I prefer—I need!—to be outside, tromping along a still half- frozen stream. Or slogging through marshland to risk my life when I don't give a fig. But the beach along the Bay heals me best.

Spring is mostly indoors. They sit, pudgy chin in pudgy hand, peering through the window, wondering what they are missing. Wipe their eyes to glimpse one sail. Is that the sweet call of the dove under an eave, or fisherman making his first catch. Children build with simple blocks on the carpet. But their boats boast bright keels—blue below and red above the waterline, candycane-striped sails, sky blue wheelhouse.

As they grow older they color on paper, their India ink lines now taking in the surface of the Bay, even contours of the shore. Piers spring up and groves of trees and faraway ridges. They leap into books which take them around the world to all different shores. They hear sea music and dance the jig, the reel, the hornpipe, the farandole. They try to warble in foreign tongues.

...Meanwhile back on the beach I trudge hard gray sand. Nothing lives except the breathing tides; a systole and diastole of coughing surf. Often sky matches ocean in tone; earth no more than mousy brown. I shake a fist at heaven, knowing underneath it is my fate and no one else's. But the bellow feels great. A fistful of sand, of Bay water, is good for the soul.

Birth is a gift and a challenge. Soon...very soon...mark me...the beach will fully live again; as the trees and grasses will. It is a long time arriving, but it will surely come.

The Moanings

The masts cry
both summer and winter,
they complain about ice
squeezing against their hulls
(praise be to bubblers)
wind gives no quarter,
but in summer they moan
to be loosed
to be gone
out of the coves
down the rivers
into open Bay and sea
to swim, to fly again.

Voices

Ironically, Virginia was born in Kentucky. She never liked her name and wanted it changed to Ginnie, because somehow it sounded friendlier. She was brilliant in high school, all A's. College was mentioned; she said it wasn't worth it.

She worked in a bank and went on vacations with her three girlfriends. She liked to play cards and smoke. Puns, parodies, impersonations flowed out of her mouth; her voice low and raspy.

When she married Mort, it was almost like an afterthought. They moved to the Bay where he started a successful little business and bought a house by the water. If anybody mentioned her having children, she said no way. He died; it seemed a very small glitch in Ginnie's afterlife.

She liked to keep her hands busy. She quilted. Even into old age she loved reading; you could glimpse her bent under a light, book in her lap, head wreathed with smoke. As she aged, she seemed somehow to appear black and white: silver hair and a wan complexion contrasted against her preferred colors of gray or dark blue.

But something new began to develop in her. She would invite a neighbor in for tea or coffee. Then she would blurt out that ESP had come suddenly to her as a great gift. She heard miraculous things: a fife and drum corps—she was sure—came from the 18th century when the town was founded. The sounds came right out of the pipes in the walls. It was like being in a time machine, she spluttered excitedly. She couldn't really control it; all she could do was note what she heard and pass it on.

Then she was seeing them too. Yes, ignorance could dismiss them as only Ginnie's very old age. Finally the house was sold. A builder bought the place, completely renovated and turned it into a show piece with its own dock and boathouse. She was put into a county home. She bothered no one, deciding to no longer speak until the day she died.

Not only sailors at sea are superstitious. So are many of those who live by the water. With a life of its own the Bay can do that.

Old Days

They would amble down
to the Bay to muse,
they would dream about
butter or bowling or boots.
Anxiety was not
then a major ailment,
sun, moon, a breeze meant a lot,
they could get along on few,
man or woman or dog.
Then simple things became
complicated and we
tangled up in our own
electronic cobwebs.

Waiting

It was a glorious, sunny summer day; low humidity, just a bit of breeze. The retired couple warmly greeted their guests, a somewhat younger couple. They stood around awkwardly in the living room until the drift of the day began to settle in. Asked if they were hungry after their long drive, they said no; the younger couple simply preferred tall glasses of cold local water.

They admired the paintings of the Bay, the six elephants; the close-up sequenced photos of the butterfly in flight, the photo of a Venetian canal which resembled a painting. Then the four walked in the garden, remarking about the reds, yellows, whites, three shades of purple against a green pine grove setting.

They decided to stroll to the first beach which had a large, open-sided shed where grilling could be done; the beach where once a water-logged piece of driftwood could not be dragged home. The second beach had a fishing pier attached; this is where colored glass was most readily found; this is where a large unidentified fish was caught. The third beach showed the foundations of a structure everyone living had no knowledge of; where some years ago a drunken man had accosted the older couple.

The last beach was reached across a log bridge that spanned a languid stream, slipping its humble share into the Bay; this public space had swings and a platform where folksingers sometimes performed; where seabirds were plentiful in the shallow tide. They stopped to dutifully read the historic plaques commemorating people and events from the Revolutionary War and the War of 1812.

At home again, they had lunch on the deck under a multi-striped umbrella: a salad, French bread, three cheeses, smoked oysters, a red and a white wine; for dessert strawberries, peaches, cherries, blueberries. They all agreed this was an ideal life.

Then they conversed into the long, mellow afternoon. They spoke of their long relationship, possibility of the younger couple's future retirement, deaths of mutual friends, bodily health, travel, books, odd happenings. They were all relaxed and laughed a lot into the summer air.

As the younger couple prepared to leave, jokingly the young husband asked the hosts what they would do until meeting again next summer. "We'll sit right here and wait for you," the older woman replied with a sad smile.

It's Spring

Our eggshell broken
we slither on our way,
our silken cocoon cracked
we flutter away;
Bay rolling again
no longer ice-chunked
to a stalled halt like
a seasonal railway strike;
beefy sky puffing out
last gray clouds, swearing
to break the habit,
switching on the longlost
and so pure blue light.

Cameos

I could talk about many more of the people who live in our village beside the Bay.

A man worked for years at a TV station as a cameraman behind the scenes. He decided to quit to become Santa Claus, a professional Santa so to speak. He had enough money to get by. He had a lovely gray-haired wife—still lovely in figure and disposition at age sixty—to give him moral support. He had the belly and full white beard; he even had business cards printed. He would perform, of course, for Christmas celebrations; also weddings, graduations, confirmations, anniversaries, Thanksgiving , if they wanted him.

A single man, a cross-country trucker, lived in a stone house in town. His large garage was also stone; as a challenge he took it apart, replacing walls with cedar shakes. He didn't know how handy with rock he could be. He put on a second floor in the garage and created an "entertainment center." With remaining rock he built walls and enclosed gardens on his half-acre. The walls were even neatly capped with slate.

The town maintenance man lived on the edge of the village in a small cabin, all windows shuttered closed. He used kerosene for lighting, heat, and cooking. One nosy soul who once peeked inside said it was clean and tidy. Although the man used electric tools in his job, he preferred a simpler life in his privacy.

Late at night lights burn in another house. A woman is a ham radio operator. At night reception is clearer so she can talk to radio friends around the world. She has never left the state and does not want to.

A man with Alzheimer's walks the beach with a metal detector in all seasons and any kind of weather. He says hello, has a little friendly talk with you, then goes on his way. If he seems lost we walk him home.

A house painter brags that he has had every hobby possible: coins, stamps, license plates, community theater, choir, watercolor—but raising passenger pigeons are his greatest delight.

I could tell you about many more of these characters, for after all haven't we sometimes done strange things, aren't we all unique? But time is running out, if I want to ever finish this book.

Spring Moment

Distant shore rouged at dusk
sky blooming in lilac cloth;
an opal from a chain
moon drops into my glass
of champagne, bubbles which
rise as in a snow globe
inverted, a tulip shape
whose stem I twirl to
stir mayhem; soon actual
tulip and lilac
scents will intoxicate
will fill the garden with
their exhilaration.

Next Door Again

Recently a nice family moved in next door. The mom works in a daycare center; she is also skilled at photography. A son who is still living home is a gardener. Another son who lives up the Bay comes over to fix their roof or siding; whatever needs doing. They are waiting for another son to come home from military duty; so far he is fine. They even started a little vegetable garden in the side yard.

They also own two pekes who look at you through the fence like guardians of the Forbidden City. They have a young setter too who, like Snoopy, stands on top of his doghouse. He got loose one day and was hit by a truck; he healed fine but now when the mother drives with him, he tries to hide under her feet.

It's also an extended family. The grandfather is a regular smurf, belly and beard and all. He is an active Mason and runs a Boy Scout troop. The grandmom is losing it a bit, can't remember things, but she sits on the front lawn talking to neighbors. We will keep our fingers crossed for them and for the future.

Old Tales

Nodding by a sea-coal fire
he imagines coastal tales
winging towards him,
but no more watermen work
the shores, the coves, the deep,
so do these sages
evaporate like
a computer site withdrawn.
Timid spring sun goes down
who knows when summer will come,
his bass voice runs ahead
of him, a pet gone wild
to echo in a corner.

Beginnings and Endings

Some American books about bodies of water have marvelous openings, such as Van Dyke's *Little Rivers* or Jewett's *Country of the Pointed Firs*. Others contain a striking closing, Michener's *Chesapeake* or Miller's *The Colossus of Marousi*. However, the reader is always on the lookout for those which present perfect bookends in both start and finish.

Here is an initial passage from John Steinbeck's *Cannery Row*: "Cannery Row in Monterey in California is a poem, a stink, a grating noise, a quality of light, a tone, a habit, a nostalgia, a dream."

And from Henry Beston's *The Outermost House*: "East and ahead of the coast of North America, some thirty miles and more from the inner shores of Massachusetts, there stands in the open Atlantic the last fragments of an ancient and vanished land. For twenty miles this last and outer earth faces the ever hostile ocean in the form of a great eroded cliff of earth and clay, the undulations and levels of whose rim now stand a hundred, now a hundred and fifty feet above the tides. Worn by the breakers and the rains, disintegrated by the wind, it still stands bold. Many earths compose it, and many gravels and sands stratified and intermingled. It has many colours: old ivory here, peat here, and here old ivory darkened and enriched with rust. At twilight, its rain lifted to the splendour in the west, the face of the wall becomes a substance of shadows and dark descending to the eternal unquiet of the sea; at dawn the sun rising out of ocean gilds it with a level silence of light which thins and rises and vanishes into day."

In his book *Cape Cod*, Henry Thoreau wrote in summation: "But this shore will never be more fashionable than it is now. Such beaches as are fashionable are here made and remade in a day, I may almost say, by the sea shifting its sands. Lynn and Nantasket! this bare and bended arm it is that makes the bay in which they lie so snugly. What are springs and waterfalls? Here is the spring of springs, the waterfall of waterfalls. A storm in the fall or winter is the time to visit it; a light-house or a fisherman's hut the true hotel. A man may stand there and put all America behind him."

And in *Gift from the Sea*, by Anne Morrow Lindbergh: "When we start at the center of ourselves, we discover something worthwhile extending toward the periphery of the circle. We find again some of the joy in the new, some of the peace in the here, some of the love in me and thee which go to make up the kingdom of heaven on earth.

The waves echo behind me. Patience—Faith—Openness, is what the sea has to teach. Simplicity—Solitude—Intermittence. But there are other beaches to explore. There are more shells to find. This is only a beginning."

Living on Graysheep Bay

My love,
our sky is filled with music,
our glass with the most
brilliant vintage,
our lips often meet as
mating butterflies yet
in a more golden light;
we have truly taken
the firmest root here
and as our garden
grows as the years do,
what we reap will only
grow richer.

About the body typeface

Adobe Caslon Pro Caslon is the name given to serif typefaces designed by William Caslon I (c. 1692–1766) in London, or inspired by his work.

Caslon worked as an engraver of punches, the masters used to stamp the moulds or matrices used to cast metal type. He worked in the tradition of what is now called old-style serif letter design, that produced letters with a relatively organic structure resembling handwriting with a pen. His typefaces established a strong reputation for their quality and their attractive appearance, suitable for extended passages of text.

Readers Guide

1. In "The Ideal Couple" how do Helen and Stewart represent many young couples today?

2. What do characters like Hap, Daisy, Chip, or Virginia represent?

3. Why is the chapter "Extermination" in letter form?

4. Do the paintings mentioned in the chapter "Art of the Bay" add to the reader's vision of the Bay?

5. "Tides" or "On the Bay" seems to be a story within a story. What is its uniqueness?

6. A list in "The Shore" seems unusual in a novel. What does it accomplish?

7. Several chapters are about events in houses in the coastal community. Choose one and talk about its relevance.

8. What do the "Daybook" chapters achieve in the overall context of the book?

9. Is there any humor in the book. Discuss.

10. The book is designed to trace the seasons through the year. Analyze.

11. In "The Gay Year" what does "the hose" symbolize?

12. Does "Town Meeting" sound like other town meetings you've heard or read about?

13. In "Waiting" is the older couple depressed?

14. Why are so many of the poems written in fragments? Why are they so short?

15. Does the poem "Into the Wooden Bowl" have any connection with the succeeding chapter "Especially Autumn?"

16. Why does the author often intrude with comments about the art of writing?

17. Where do you see the Bay influencing the people who live near it?

www.ingramcontent.com/pod-product-compliance
Lightning Source LLC
Chambersburg PA
CBHW020405030726
47496CB00007B/2305